The

A royal kingdom, three beautiful princesses and three handsome suitors...

For Lanza, Donetta and Fausta Rossiano, princesses of Domodossola, duty comes first and love comes second. So when their father, King Victor Alonso, decides to step down from the throne, it's time for these royal sisters to get married!

But whether they run away, make a marriage of convenience or have a fake engagement, it's not long before these gorgeous royals find that love and marriage really do go together!

Discover Lanza's story in

The Princess's New Year Wedding

And read Donetta's story in

The Prince's Forbidden Bride

Both available now!

Look out for Fausta's story

Coming soon!

Dear Reader,

I was a typical little girl who loved fairy tales. My mother would take me and my four sisters to the library and we would check out as many books as we could. I adored anything to do with princesses, princes, magic spells, castles, crowns and jewels. But I read them too fast and had to wait until she took us to the library a week later to get more. I never had enough reading material, so I would sit on the radiator cover by the window in the living room for hours drawing pictures of a princess in a beautiful gown, or I would use tracing paper to copy some of my favorite pictures out of the books.

One of my favorite stories was *The Twelve Dancing Princesses*. I'd dream about the different kinds of princes who danced with them after midnight. That story stayed with me all my life and was the inspiration for my The Princess Brides series. But instead of twelve, I chose three of the king's daughters and fractured their traditional tale by turning everything around. I won't tell you how, but I hope you like my flight of fancy in this second book, *The Prince's Forbidden Bride*.

Enjoy!

Rebecca Winters

The Prince's Forbidden Bride

Rebecca Winters

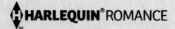
HARLEQUIN® ROMANCE

Recycling programs
for this product may
not exist in your area.

ISBN-13: 978-1-335-49938-7

The Prince's Forbidden Bride

First North American publication 2019

HARLEQUIN®

™ www.Harlequin.com

Printed in U.S.A.

Rebecca Winters lives in Salt Lake City, Utah. With canyons and high alpine meadows full of wildflowers, she never runs out of places to explore. They, plus her favorite vacation spots in Europe, often end up as backgrounds for her romance novels—because writing is her passion, along with her family and church. Rebecca loves to hear from readers. If you wish to email her, please visit her website at rebeccawinters.net.

Books by Rebecca Winters

Harlequin Romance

Visit the Author Profile page
at Harlequin.com for more titles.

How lucky was I to be born to my darling, talented mother, who was beautiful inside and out? She filled my life with joy and made me so happy to be alive! I love you, Mom.

Praise for
Rebecca Winters

PROLOGUE

A TRUMPET SOUNDED, followed by the voice of the announcer.

"This year's winner in the sixteen-year-olds' jumping and dressage, in the junior division of the Emerian *concorso*, is Princess Donetta Rossiano of the country of Domodossola. Congratulations to this unparalleled equestrian and her horse, Blaze!"

Everyone in the crowd clapped with enthusiasm.

"She has been the reigning international champion in these events since her first appearance at the Windsor *concorso*, when she was ten years old and accompanied by her father, King Victor of Domodossola. Today she's accompanied by her trainer, her father's cousin, Prince Lorenzo, a world-famous equestrian in his own right."

There was more clapping.

"And now Her Royal Highness, Queen Anne of Emeria, will present the winner's cup."

Donetta was overjoyed to have won, but she was even more excited to receive her prize from the queen. The elegant young monarch was so lucky to be born in a country where she *could* be queen.

Being the eldest of three daughters, Donetta had always dreamed of being queen of Domodossola one day. Somehow she would make it happen. Even if the law didn't allow women to rule, she was determined to find a way to get it changed.

Prince Lorenzo stood next to her. "You deserved to win the overall championship because you're the best! I knew you would do it. Too bad your family couldn't be here. They would be very proud."

"Thanks, Lorenzo, but I'm glad you're here. You're the expert who taught me how to ride. You deserve a prize, too." Lorenzo had won many awards in *concorsos* throughout his youth.

Donetta was secretly thrilled he'd come. Lorenzo, who also served as her chaperone on these trips, always gave her the freedom to have fun at the different *concorsos* without following her around, something she needed badly today.

"If Princess Donetta will please come forward to the dais."

"Go claim your well-deserved prize," Lorenzo whispered.

A round of applause accompanied her walk to the table, where pictures were taken of her with the queen. When Queen Anne handed Donetta the cup, she whispered, "You're the most outstanding female rider I've ever seen, Princess Donetta. I expect to hear of more exciting victories on that remarkable horse."

"Thank you, Your Majesty. This is a great privilege for me."

Donetta could only imagine doing this same thing for a young rider one day when *she* was queen.

She carried the engraved silver cup back to her spot in line with Lorenzo, treasuring the moment.

Another trumpet sounded, followed by the next announcement.

"This year's male winner in the sixteen-year-old division is a name we've been applauding since he first rode his horse at the Windsor *concorso* at the age of ten. Prince Enrico of the country of Vallefiore, riding his horse, Rajah! If you'll come forward to the dais, Queen Anne will present your international winner's cup."

The prince stood next to his first cousin Prince Giovanni. Giovanni had lost his parents in a plane crash, and after introducing him to Donetta, Enrico explained that his parents had taken over raising Giovanni. He lived at the palace with Enrico and his family. The two were like brothers and did everything together. Donetta had liked Giovanni immediately.

As her gaze riveted on Enrico, he flashed her a glance that said he was equally excited to see her and be with her again. They had plans when this was over. If her fifteen-year-old sister Fausta were here, she would say he was so dreamy he looked like a movie star.

He was *more* than dreamy.

Six years ago the prince had caught Donetta's ten-year-old eye when she'd first watched him perform at Windsor in his division. Even at the age of ten, he'd been a little taller and stronger than the other male contestants of his age. With his olive skin and dark hair, he'd definitely been the best looking.

Back then she'd noticed everything about him, from his penetrating black-fringed eyes to his outstanding performance on his splendid black horse, Malik. She'd envied the way the two were so tuned in to each other; it was as if they were one.

To Donetta's surprise, Enrico had sought her out after the prizes had been awarded. He'd complimented her on the way she rode and she'd returned the praise. From then on, whenever they saw each other at the dozen *concorsos* held every year in various countries, they would try to spend time together. No one else existed for them. They would discuss the finer points of each other's performances and talk about their lives.

Because of Enrico's striking looks and intelligence, Donetta never noticed the other male contestants. Whenever she learned he was on the list of competitors for his age group, her eyes always sought his and he'd find her once the competition was over.

They'd walk off away from the others.

Often they hid out on the grounds to talk and laugh. From that first *concorso*, she lived for each meeting.

Today, as Donetta watched him accept his silver cup, she realized he was becoming a man, one whose looks and charisma had a visceral effect on her.

Donetta examined her heart and realized she had an infatuation for Enrico that wasn't about to go away.

Now that his presentation was over, the groups disbanded and she handed her silver cup to Lorenzo, who would be staying to talk to the officials.

He smiled at her. "I'll see you at the entrance in an hour?"

"That's perfect. Thank you!"

In a quiet voice he said, "I know why you've always been so excited to ride in every *concorso* possible, and I've kept a blind eye. Have fun, but be careful and remember—you've been promised to Prince Arnaud. Need I remind you that the Rossianos and the Montedoros have been in a feud over trade rights for two hundred years. If your parents ever find out about you and Prince Enrico…"

"Don't worry. I'm always careful and I know you won't tell." None of his warnings bothered her a bit. She was excited to be with Enrico. They loved being together whenever they could, especially knowing it was forbidden by their two families.

Now was her chance to get away and be alone with him. She started walking her horse toward the stable, knowing he would catch up.

"Donetta?"

She trembled as that seductive voice did unexpected things to her, but she didn't want people to know she was waiting for him. It was always better if he was the one who approached her. Her legs felt less substantial as she turned to him.

"Enrico!" She was so excited to see him she could hardly stand it.

"Congratulations! You gave a superb performance!"

"I wanted to tell you the same thing, but we can't talk here. How about we both mount our horses and take a ride away from the track?"

Donetta wanted to be with him all day. Right now she was too eager to spend time with him to worry about an ancient feud, or her parents' plan that she marry Arnaud one day. Enrico's parents had promised him to Princess Valentina of Vallefiore one day, but like Donetta, he didn't give it any thought.

They walked to the stable. She found her horse's stall, where her groomsman had brought Blaze after her last event. "I'll meet you here after you've retrieved Rajah. We'll have to ride bareback."

A smile broke out on his handsome face. "Do me one favor? Don't wear your helmet." His eyes played over her features, sending a thrill of excitement through her body.

She chuckled. "Why?"

"Because for once I'd like to see your hair completely uncovered." On that unexpected note he strode away from her on his long, powerful legs. No guy could look better in riding breeches than he did. At six-two, he was becoming a man.

His comment had caused her to tremble. She removed her Devon riding jacket and helmet. After shaking her head to loosen her hair, she walked over to Blaze and offered him a treat and gave him a hug.

"You were brilliant today. I love you. How

would you like to take me for a ride without the saddle? We're going on a walk with Rajah."

She removed the trappings and her devoted horse nudged her. "Ah...that feels good, doesn't it?"

Donetta reached for the reins and mounted him. No more competition today. No more rules. Just pure fun with the most gorgeous guy she'd ever known. For him to have asked her to go riding with him on this special day made her happier than she'd ever been in her life.

As they backed out, she saw Enrico without his helmet, coming on his stallion. Normally they didn't allow stallions to enter the competitions, but it seemed they'd made an exception for the prince in this competition. He had total control over his animal.

Enrico, too, had shed his jacket and had loosened his white show shirt at the throat. When they walked out into the sun, the rays glistened on his luxuriant black hair.

Donetta's willingness to ride bareback was one of the reasons Enrico found it so exhilarating to be with the princess. Her spirit of adventure made her different from all the other princesses his family forced him to spend time with.

None of them could ride the way she did or be more entertaining. As his best friend and first cousin Prince Giovanni had been saying since they'd been coming to the *concorsos* together, Princess Donetta was poetry in motion, on or off her mare.

Her five-foot-seven-inch height gave her a regal elegance that had nothing to do with her title. In her navy-and-beige riding kit she looked spectacular, especially with her silvery gold hair cascading down her shoulders and back, shining like one of the waterfalls secreted in the mountains of Vallefiore.

She'd been very pretty, but now with those shimmering light green eyes that reminded him of the South Seas he'd seen in his travels, she'd turned into a raving beauty. Whenever he saw her in a crowd—always surrounded by more males than females—he couldn't take his eyes off her.

"You rode a new horse today, Enrico. Why did you name him Rajah?"

Her question brought him back to the present. "To befit his kingly Arabian ancestry. His breed runs wild on the plains in my country and his instincts are phenomenal."

"I'd love to see a sight like that. He's absolutely gorgeous. With him you'll continue to win every competition from now on."

"I'm sure you will, too. No other rider comes close to you."

She beamed as he led them on a path away from the track to the park in the distance. When they reached the trees, they dismounted. "I brought a picnic for us."

"You're kidding!"

Enrico pulled a blanket out of his saddlebag and spread it on the ground. Then he produced several sacks of sandwiches, fruit and drinks.

"This is fabulous, Enrico." She sat down with him to eat.

"Much as I want to spend the entire weekend with you, that isn't possible. I'd give anything if we were eighteen. Then I'd be able to take you to an early dinner and dancing in some trendy café. But we're not old enough to go out to a place like that yet."

"No. My parents would never allow it. What about you?"

"I could steal away with you now if I

could, but since that isn't possible, we'll have to wait until we're eighteen. Then we'll do whatever we want. You're the only girl I want to be with."

"I think about you all the time."

He darted her a penetrating glance. "You don't know the half of it. As soon as we turn eighteen, we'll go out after every *concorso*. That's a promise. In the meantime we'll have to make do with picnics."

"Next time it will be my turn to bring the food. I'll manage it somehow." She glanced at her watch and moaned. "I'd better go back. Lorenzo gave me an hour."

"What would happen if you're two hours late?"

"I don't dare test him and find out."

"I was just teasing, but it doesn't mean I can't dream."

"I know. I feel the same way."

He got to his feet and cleaned up the mess. After putting everything back in the saddle-bag, they returned to the stable.

Frustrated that they had to part, Enrico dismounted in front of Blaze's stall. "I'll help you down." He held out his arms. "I won't let you fall."

Donetta glanced at him again with that enticing smile. "I'm sure I can trust you." She reached for him. The second he felt her in his arms, he pulled her against him before lowering her to the ground. Every beautiful part of her fit perfectly, increasing his desire for her.

"I'm going to miss seeing you, let alone our talks, Donetta." Unable to help himself, he lowered his head to kiss her mouth, knowing he wouldn't be able to be with her until the next *concorso*. She tasted so good he couldn't stop and began kissing her long and hard, sweeping them away until both were breathless. This kiss would have to last.

Sometime later he unwillingly released her. "Until next time. Have a safe flight home, *bellissima*," he murmured before reaching for his horse's reins to walk away.

Two years later, there'd been twenty more horse competitions where Donetta had met with Enrico. They'd enjoyed picnics and kissed each other until they were breathless. Now that they had both turned eighteen, Donetta was dying to be with Enrico again because they could really be together now for hours and hours.

After she won the overall championship for eighteen-year-olds at the *concorso* in Vienna, she'd worked it out with Lorenzo to look the other way while she and Enrico went out to dinner. She promised to be back at their hotel by 11:00 p.m., and Giovanni had hired a limo for them.

Donetta almost died with happiness when Enrico took her to a club where they could have dinner and dance. He never let her out of his arms, kissing her cheek and neck.

"You don't know how long I've waited for this, Donetta."

"Oh, yes, I do! Thank heaven there's another *concorso* next month, otherwise I'm not going to be able to handle the separation."

He kissed her lips before dancing them back to their table. It was already getting to be eleven o'clock, but she didn't care. She wanted to stay out all night with him.

"Donetta," he said after they sat down. "There's something I have to tell you, but I'm dreading it."

Some nuance in his voice told her she wasn't going to like it. "What's wrong?"

"Today was my last time to ride in a *concorso.*"

She blinked. "What are you talking about? We can ride in competitions until we're a lot older. I don't understand."

He gripped her hand across the table. "Next week I'm leaving for England to attend university at Cambridge. Giovanni will be going with me. I won't be riding in any competitions from now on. There's no time. During the next four years I'll be spending most of my time studying. There'll be a few visits to see my family."

Donetta had been so drunk with happiness the import of his statement took a minute to sink in. "I see," she said in a quiet voice. "What will you study?"

"Business, law enforcement, finance, economics, agriculture."

"I'm envious."

"Aren't you going to be attending college, too?"

"Yes. Next month, but it won't be in England. My parents insist I get my education at Domodossola University. They don't want me going far away."

"I wish you could come to Cambridge, where we could spend all our free time together after our classes are over, to study and do *other* things…" His words caught at her heart. "Will you be competing in more *concorsos* while you're at university?"

By now they'd been served dessert, but she couldn't touch hers. "Maybe some of them."

"After the performance you put on today, I have no doubt you'll continue to win everything. I heard what the head of the Austrian federation said to you after your win. Your ability on a horse is breathtaking."

"Thank you," she said, trying to smile, but her heart was heavy.

"It's killing me that I won't see you again."

Enrico squeezed her hand harder. "I know I've upset you. Now you have some idea of what the separation's going to do to me."

Tears flooded her eyes. "The thought of not seeing you again… I can't handle it. Your presence has always made the competitions more exciting for me. Everyone asks, is Prince Enrico going to win again? They think I know. And I do," she said with a teasing smile.

"Now you're really flattering me. I'll watch for your name in the competitions coming up on the lists in the next few years and try to get away to see you."

"Oh, please come!"

"I don't want to lose you, Donetta. In the meantime let's write to each other. I'll send you letters through your equestrian foundation and ask Giovanni to mail them."

She brightened. "I'll do the same through your organization and put Prince Giovanni's name on the envelope so he'll send them on to you. No one will be able to monitor them. Our families will be incensed if they find out that a Montedoro and a Rossiano have been carrying on a forbidden relationship all these years."

"You're right. That old ridiculous animosity over trade rights between our two countries is still a sore spot with my family. But I refuse to worry about that right now."

"I've never worried about it," Donetta said with stunning honesty. Neither of them had talked about the people they were promised to. Both sets of parents would be enraged about what had been going on behind the scenes.

"Much as I don't want to, I'd better get you back to the hotel. Lorenzo will be looking for you, and Giovanni will be waiting for me at the airport. We're flying home on the royal jet tonight."

That revelation brought more pain to her heart as they left the club in the limo.

"Come closer, Donetta. I don't want to waste one second of the precious time we have left." He pulled her into his arms and kissed the daylights out of her until the limo pulled up in front of the hotel.

He finally let her go. "I'll write to you as soon as I'm in England. Stay safe and send me some pictures."

"I'll be waiting for your letters and pictures, too."

They embraced one more time before he helped her out of the limo. She ran inside the hotel, where Lorenzo was waiting for her.

He looked at his watch. "You're only a half hour late. I can forgive you for that."

She hugged him hard. "Thank you for being my friend."

"Why the tears?"

"I've had some disappointing news, but today was the best day of my life."

Dear Donetta,
When you told me you were participating in the concorso at Aix-en-Provence in France, I bought this book for your

twenty-first birthday. It tells the history of the white Camargue horses of that region. I believe you'll find it fascinating.

I plan to fly in for your competition and will be staying at the Hotel Cezanne, where you are staying. I'll ring your room.

We'll spend as much time together as we can while I'm there. I'm longing to see you again. All the letters and photos have kept me going, but it's been a century since I kissed you.
Enrico

After reading the book from cover to cover, Donetta kissed Enrico's letter. It traveled to her purse, her pocket and her pillow. She had it with her when she entered the hotel. This time her staff stayed at a different hotel. So did Lorenzo, who'd flown here with her but had come only to watch her perform, not keep tabs on her.

Once she was in her room, her pulse raced and wouldn't subside, because she knew she'd be seeing Enrico shortly. She had brought several outfits with her, not knowing what to wear. After much indecision she chose to wear a filmy short-sleeved dress in champagne color and bone-colored sandals.

To please him Donetta left her hair long and flowing from a side part. After applying pink, frosted lipstick, she put on hoop earrings of the same light green color as her eyes. She wanted him to take one look at her and never let her go.

When the room phone rang, she literally jumped before picking up.

"H-Hello?" she stammered.

"Thank heaven your voice hasn't changed."

His had grown even deeper. "Neither has yours."

"Are you ready?"

"Yes," she answered, almost out of breath.

"Meet me in the lobby in five minutes. I've rented a car. We're going to take off and find a charming spot away from the world where we can be alone."

Donetta came close to fainting when she saw the man of her dreams standing near the entrance, wearing a tan suit and sports shirt. No man came close to her picture of Enrico, who was the personification of every woman's dream of a dark-haired prince. At almost twenty-two, he was truly breathtaking and sensuously male.

"Bellissima," he murmured. His black eyes played over her hungrily before he grasped her hand. They walked to the parking area and got in his car. He drove them out of the city to the suburbs and pulled up to a place called the Patio.

"Before we get out, I have to do this."

"Enrico—" she cried as he reached for her and his mouth closed over hers. It didn't seem possible that she was in his arms again and they were giving each other kiss for kiss, unable to get enough.

Evening turned into night as they tried to make up for the years when they hadn't been able to be together. The letters and photos hadn't been enough.

"If you're dying for dinner, we'll get out of the car, but I don't want to let you go."

She shook her head. "I'm only dying for you. After your letter and gift, which I love, I haven't been able to concentrate on anything. All I want is to be with you."

"We're safer here than back at the hotel, where everyone knows us. But this is no way for us to have a relationship. One more year of schooling for both of us and then we can make plans to be together. What if we take a trip after we graduate? How about two weeks to the South Seas or a Caribbean island?"

"I'd give anything to go away with you. Anything!"

"Then we'll do it. You're so beautiful, Donetta, I think I'm hallucinating. Kiss me again."

After another half hour they ended up driving to a store for fruit and some quiche. "I need to get us back to the hotel. You're performing in the morning and need your sleep."

"No, I don't. I only need you."

The car was their sanctuary. They didn't go into the hotel until after one. "I'd come to your room, but then you'd never get rid of me and we'd be the target of every eye. I'll be at the stands in the morning to watch you on Blaze."

They rode the elevator to the second floor, where he had to get out, but they clung to each other.

"Enrico? How soon do you have to get back to Cambridge?"

"Tomorrow night."

"Why don't we just drive away right now until you have to be at the airport. I'll skip the competition."

He pressed his forehead against hers. "You can't do that. I can't let you. But we'll be together all day tomorrow." Enrico let her go and stepped out into the hall. He looked back. "Meet me in the lobby at seven and we'll go somewhere for breakfast before you have to report to the stands."

"Don't go, Enrico. I'm afraid."

He frowned. "Why do you say that?"

"Because I'm too happy."

"You don't know the meaning of the word yet. *Buona notte e sogni d' oro*, Donetta."

Golden dreams. She'd been living in one since they'd met in the lobby. "*Buona notte*, Enrico."

The elevator door closed and carried her to the third floor. When she reached her room, the phone was ringing. She rushed to answer it. "Enrico?"

"Good. You're home safe and sound for tonight. I'll be dreaming of you."

"I dream of you every night," she confessed.

"One of these days we won't have to do that anymore."

He clicked off.

She was slower to hang up. If he meant what she thought he'd meant, he wasn't just talking about a two-week vacation. Filled with elation, she whirled around the room before settling down long enough to undress and get to bed.

CHAPTER ONE

THERE WAS NO sight more beautiful to Crown Prince Enrico da Francesca di Montedoro than the island country of Vallefiore. In the early morning light, the sun's first rays appeared like fingers over the magnificent vertiginous mountains and sparkling waterfalls.

From his vantage point atop the highest peak, he could see his country was surrounded by the deep blue waters of the Ionian Sea splashing against rocky shoreline cliffs and hidden grottoes.

He'd always likened his country to a dazzling blue-green jewel whose lakes and villages made up its many facets, including the plains where the wild Sanfratellano horses ran free.

His eyes followed the lay of the land over rolling hills and orchards to palm-studded sand. Everything could grow here in its subtropical climate. But as his father, King Nuncio, had told Enrico when he was a boy, without more fresh water to irrigate, it couldn't flourish as it should.

From that day on, Enrico had a dream that one day he'd find a way to bring much-needed water to all parts of the eleven-thousand-square-mile island. Now, at the age of twenty-seven, he and his cousin Giovanni, always his best friend and now his personal assistant, were slowly fulfilling that dream.

Today he'd come to the topmost point of the new water treatment plant to talk to the foreman, Giuseppe, and work out a few small problems. They talked for several hours and discussed the results of the huge project he and Giovanni had developed. At this point other countries wanted to adopt it.

After saying goodbye to the foreman, he climbed back in his Land Rover, surrounded by his bodyguards. He headed down the mountain for the palace in Saracene an hour away. The capital city was located on Lake Saracene, the large, brilliant light green body of water resembling those in the tropics.

Donetta possessed eyes that same color.

He remembered the last time he'd looked into them before kissing her senseless. Those two days in Aix-en-Provence had been heaven. She'd once again won another competition, filling him with pride. He'd come close to kidnapping her for good before he came to his senses.

Consumed with ideas for the two of them after graduation, he'd returned to Cambridge more anxious than ever to finish his studies and fulfill his desire to be with her on a permanent basis.

But right before his graduation, his world had come close to falling apart when he'd learned the tragic news that his father had been diagnosed with Alzheimer's and his mother needed him. He had to fly home immediately and forgo his graduation ceremony.

What made the situation worse was his mother's insistence that the palace keep the world in the dark over the king's diagnosis. She didn't want the citizenry to learn that the disease had taken over completely and he could no longer function. This meant Enrico was forced to settle into his duties as crown prince the second the jet touched down.

Enrico was put under further pressure when his mother arranged for Valentina to be a visitor to the palace. The queen was demanding he marry her. Both sets of parents had been good friends for years and she expected Enrico to propose immediately. At the time of the marriage, an official coronation would make Enrico king. Only then would it be revealed that King Nuncio was ill.

Enrico had no intention of marrying Valentina, but the visits had been captured in the news, creating the excitement of a coming royal wedding for the country. To end this nightmare, he'd told his mother there would be no wedding in the foreseeable future while he was attempting to run the affairs of the kingdom.

His desire to take Donetta on a two-week trip had been thwarted by circumstances beyond his control. In his next letter to her, he told her the vacation would have to be put off and he wouldn't be writing any letters for a while.

Without giving away the secret about his father, he explained his work for the country had become too involved. When the time came, he would get in touch with her again.

He'd received a response that said she understood how busy he must be and hoped to see him again soon. "I miss you, Enrico." He could hear her voice that tugged on his heart. That was the last letter from her.

Now it was five years later and he still couldn't stop thinking about her and wishing they could meet again. Did she still miss him? How would they really feel about each other after such a long absence?

At the age of eighteen Enrico had already made up his mind over the woman he wanted in his life. In his wildest fantasy he'd even dreamed of Donetta becoming his bride, despite knowing such a marriage would raise a furor with their families.

Because of the two-hundred-year-old dispute that had made their countries enemies, Enrico had never told anyone about her except his cousin. But not even Giovanni knew the extent of Enrico's feelings.

Enrico needed to find out how much of their relationship had been driven by rebellion, and how much had been based on a genuine and deep love for the each other. Ever since he'd competed on one of his special horses in an international *concorso ippico* held in England, he'd admired Princess Donetta Rossiano's ability in the dressage event.

For a ten-year-old she was a marvel, much better than any of the guys on all the teams represented from around the world. He'd approached to tell her so and was struck by the shimmering green color of her eyes, which had grown fierier as she'd matured.

She, in turn, had complimented him and had admired his horse. As they'd talked, she'd asked lots of questions about the breed he'd chosen, revealing her exceptional intelligence.

Enjoying her company, he'd spent time with her at the various tracks after each *concorso*. He liked being with her when she trained before an event. Drawn to her like crazy, he'd laughed and flirted. Her discipline and composure made Donetta stand out from the others. He'd been fascinated.

Over the years Enrico had watched the beautiful princess from Domodossola with the long, flowing silvery gold hair compete in dozens of *concorsos* just as he had. By the age of twenty-one she was all grown up, with a keen intellect and opinions on subjects that kept him riveted. On top of everything else she was the best jumper and by far the most stunning young woman he'd ever seen or known.

There was no woman like her and he *had* to see her again. Although she no longer competed in *concorsos*, she now ran the equestrian organization for her country's entrants.

A month ago Giovanni had suggested Enrico travel with him to Madrid, Spain, to watch their country's participants and horses perform in the day's events. Though Donetta might not be there, Enrico made the decision to go anyway.

It was late in the day when he finally caught sight of her near the stable. At least he thought it was Donetta, but wasn't sure until she turned around to talk to someone. To his shock she'd cut her long, diaphanous hair. It had been styled to form a feather cut that framed her beautiful face.

One look and he knew his attraction for the five-foot-seven blonde beauty had only intensified over the years. His pulse rate accelerated. When she saw him, her fabulous green eyes darkened with emotion.

"Enrico—"

"It's been five years, Donetta." Thank heaven there was no ring on her finger.

She smiled, but the element of excitement was missing in her eyes. "Now we're all grown up."

Yes, they were. Her womanly figure took his breath away.

"Your Sanfratellano horses are still making winners out of your riders."

He cocked his dark head. "It appears your country is celebrating another champion, too, but she didn't ride like you did at the *concorso* in Aix. I'll never forget our time together." Nor the way she'd filled his arms during those two days in France. "How long are you going to be in Madrid?"

"I should have left five minutes ago. The limo is waiting to take me to the airport as we speak."

Her answer came as a huge disappointment. "You have to leave right now? When I saw your country's name on the list for this competition, I came specifically to see you."

By the way she held herself taut, he knew this meeting had shaken her as much as it had him. "Knowing how busy you've been helping your father run the country, I'm surprised you could get away."

He sucked in his breath. "I deserved that,

Donetta. If we could go out to dinner and have some private time together, I need to apologize to you for so many things."

She shook her head. "I didn't say that to be mean-spirited. You don't owe me anything, Enrico. We were young, we had our fling behind our parents' backs. Those years were magical for me, but we both knew our real destiny was still out there waiting for us. But I have to admit I was shocked when you stopped writing. It hurt more than you know to realize that day had come for you."

"There were reasons," he whispered.

"You think I don't know that?" She let out an audible sigh. "I'm glad to see you again. It's such a surprise. You look wonderful."

"So do you, *bellissima*. I'd give anything if you didn't have to go yet."

"I'm sorry, but my staff is waiting for me and we're on a tight schedule. I'm grateful you came. Seeing you has given me closure. *Addio per sempre*, Enrico."

Goodbye for good? If she thought that, she had another think coming.

He watched her walk away on those long, slender legs until he couldn't see her anymore. Damn if she wasn't more gorgeous than any woman had a right to be.

Enrico had admired Donetta through a boy's eyes, but now he was a twenty-seven-year-old man and recognized those feelings for her had taken root at an early age. They'd never gone away.

No matter how bad his father's Alzheimer's had become, it was time to do something about the way he still felt about Donetta. But Madrid hadn't been the place to reconnect. She'd dropped an impenetrable shield around herself, with good reason.

He needed time and privacy so she couldn't dismiss him, because that was exactly what she'd done. It was his fault. By ending the letter writing at the time, he'd left her to believe he'd gone on to follow the path his parents had outlined for him. Enrico couldn't blame her for anything and needed to start over again with her.

On the flight back to Vallefiore with Giovanni, Enrico broke his silence over coffee and confided his long-held secret to his cousin. "I fell for Donetta when she was only ten years old. I would have married her after college if Papà hadn't already been so ill and needed me."

His cousin nodded. "I suspected *that* was the reason for all the letter writing. But the queen would never allow such a marriage. As if the bitter enmity between our two countries weren't reason enough, I'm afraid she's going to have a coronary when you don't marry Valentina."

"It's *my* life. I want Donetta. Always have. Seeing her again has let me know she's the one for me."

"Have you said as much to her?"

"Not in so many words."

Giovanni sat forward. "Why not?"

"I intend to the next time I see her."

"Next time? Did she ever admit she was in love with you?"

"No. If she had, I would have run away with her." He'd hoped to hear those words when they'd been in Spain, but they hadn't come, probably because Donetta was wary of him. Deep down it had bothered him. "Why are you asking me all these questions?"

"Because I'm afraid I have bad news for you about her."

"What do you mean? I've kept track of her

and I know she's not married yet." Enrico had always followed news about her and her family. Today he had the proof she wasn't attached to any man. Not yet…

"That's true, but you're still out of luck."

"Stop speaking in riddles."

Giovanni's eyes were as black as Enrico's. "You could never have married her."

"What are you saying?"

"I hate to tell you this, but I have it on the best authority that Princess Donetta has turned down every proposal ever received because she never plans to marry!"

Enrico shook his head. "Come on, Giovanni. It's me you're talking to."

"Don't I know it, so you *have* to take me seriously. Get this—she's living for the day when Domodossola's laws of succession change to allow women to rule. She wants to be queen."

"That could never happen."

"You and I know that. Nevertheless, up to this point in time she has wanted to reign and reign *alone*. No husband. That's why she's our age and still single!"

With that explanation, Enrico burst into laughter. That didn't sound like the Donetta who'd shared her feelings with him on paper. What he'd just heard was ridiculous, and yet it wasn't beyond possible that she did want to change her country's rules established over centuries. Besides her brains and beauty, she was the most unique woman he'd ever known.

The woman did have strong opinions that excited him, but he had no idea she was so ambitious.

"Tell me, Giovanni. How do you know all this?"

"Because I have a secret, too. As you know, your father put me in charge of the Sanfratellano Horses Federation when I was only twenty. He wanted our country to have a presence at all the international *concorsos*."

Enrico nodded. "I told him you should be the head since you knew the most about them. It made me very happy when you accepted the position."

Giovanni had been the right person to head their lucrative horse breeding business unique to the island. The Montedoro family had been renowned for over a thousand years for their fabulous Sanfratellano horses, which boasted a distinguished pedigree. They brought buyers to their stable from all over the world.

"I was happy about it, too. Once college was behind us, I got busy planning the schedule for our country's participation in more competitions when I wasn't helping you. As you know, I traveled to the various *concorsos* on the list and met Princess Fausta Rossiano in Paris last fall at a competition."

"Donetta's sister was there?"

"Yes. She came with their aunt and Donetta, who was in charge of her country's entrants. From what I've been told, the two sisters are thick as thieves. They look a lot alike. I guess our Montedoro genes are tuned into a certain type of woman. Fausta is a knockout, too."

"I agree," Enrico said.

"Naturally I wanted to get to know her better. But her best friend, Mia Giancarlo, whose father is an international banker I've worked with, gave me some private info about the two sisters that was fascinating."

"Go on."

"Mia told me that Fausta won't date any royals and would refuse to go out with me. It seems she has turned down many royal proposals because—get this—she plans to marry a commoner!"

"Are you putting me on?" Enrico demanded.

"I swear not. That's when Mia told me that Donetta has refused to marry for the reasons I just explained. It seems the only normal sister is the youngest one, Princess Lanza. She's now married to Prince Stefano of Umbriano,"

"That's right." A whistle escaped Enrico's lips.

But Enrico wouldn't allow this gossip to thwart him. In his gut he knew Donetta had loved him. He was determined to pursue her at any cost. Giovanni had given him enough information to offer her something she wouldn't be able to turn down.

"I'm going to create a situation where we can be legitimately together so I can propose. The truth is, I can't get her out of my head. I've been a fool to pretend to be doing my duty when all these years she's been the one."

"I guess if anyone can try to persuade her, it's you. But you're forgetting your mother. She'll forbid it."

"I'll remind Mamma that she had her op-

portunity to reject or accept my father's proposal when the time came. Now it's my turn."

"Good luck with that."

It was evening when they arrived at the
palace grounds and parked outside the west
wing. Their bodyguards followed in another
car. He and Giovanni shared a suite of offices
where he could get busy plotting before they
went to their own apartments to sleep.

"I've come up with a solution to get her
here, Giovanni. Don't go to bed yet. Our
country has never hosted a *concorso*. What
do you say we plan the most spectacular event
ever put on in any country? I realize it will
take time and effort, but it will be worth it."

A long silence ensued while his cousin
eyed him through narrowed lids. "You crafty
devil."

"How are you feeling on this beautiful July
day, Papà?" Twenty-seven-year-old Donetta
had served herself breakfast at the huntboard
in the small dining room of the palace and
sat down at the table with her parents and
sister Fausta.

"I'm fine."

"Are you?" She flashed her mother a

glance for verification. Her father had a heart condition he'd finally admitted to after their youngest sister Lanza had gotten married to Prince Stefano of Umbriano on New Year's Day.

"He's upset that Stefano had to fly to Argentina over mining business yesterday," Fausta explained. "Papà doesn't know how long he'll be gone, and this time Lanza went with him."

Lanza had been their father's pet forever, but since marrying Stefano, she went everywhere she could with her husband. Lanza's childhood crush on Stefano had turned into a love he reciprocated. They were crazy about each other, but their father missed her and didn't seem as happy these days.

"He *had* to go," Donetta reasoned. "What's really troubling you?"

Her father, King Victor of the country of Domodossola, looked down and frowned. "Since their wedding, Stefano has been much busier running his mining interests than I thought he'd be."

Donetta could have told him as much. Her father had hoped his new son-in-law would take over a lot of the responsibilities of governing, but Prince Stefano was a gold mining engineer. He'd brought much-needed funds to his country of Umbriano in the Alps, and now to their Kingdom of Domodossola on the French-Swiss-Italian border.

Marrying her younger sister Lanza hadn't changed what he did for a living, even though he tried to give their father as much of his time as he could when he was home.

"So why don't you lean on me while he's gone?" Donetta knew her plea would fall on deaf ears, but she said it anyway.

Her dream had always been to rule Domodossola on her own when her father no longer could, but the law of succession didn't allow a woman to rule. She'd been forced to give that dream up a long time ago.

"I can manage the latest contracts on the timber we're shipping to Umbriano." Among her college courses she'd taken finance and accounting.

He shook his head. "You're sweet, but I've got Giulio working on them." Except that their financial advisor was eighty-two and had started making mistakes.

She finished her coffee. "In that case, I'll ask you to excuse me while I go to my office."

"Don't leave yet," her father said unexpectedly. "Your mother and I have something vital to discuss with you."

She lowered her head. That could mean only one thing. *Marriage*. What else? How many times in her life had they brought it up to her!

"We've received half a dozen invitations from Prince Arnaud's family, asking that you'll spend time with them. Just last week another request came from the royal family pleading with all of us to visit their estate at Haute Vienne. It's time. You can't avoid it any longer!"

"Please take this seriously, Donetta," her mother begged her. "When they came to Lanza's wedding in January, Prince Arnaud spoke to your father and me in private. Since being with you in Paris while Fausta was there, traveling with your Zia Ottavia, he's most anxious for the betrothal to take place. The man is entranced by you, darling. You have to do something about it!"

"I'm not ready yet, Mamma." She'd found Arnaud attractive and realized that she appealed to him. But in her heart of hearts she knew that Arnaud wasn't in love with her any more than she was with him. If he weren't a royal, he would be free to choose the woman he desired.

"You said that to us a year ago, darling. Arnaud has been very patient," her mother declared. "He told me he's never wanted to marry anyone else since he met you."

"It's true," Fausta interjected. "Arnaud couldn't take his eyes off you."

Maybe so, but Fausta knew where Donetta's true heart lay and was angry at Enrico for dropping her sister.

The one man who'd stayed away five years.

Donetta loved Fausta for being so loyal and listening to her while she'd suffered over that first year after the letters stopped coming. At first she'd imagined Enrico's family had learned about the letters and his liaison with a Rossiano. In their fury, they'd demanded he break things off immediately.

Whatever the explanation, that had been the blackest, bleakest time in her life and only in the last year had she managed to pull out of the pain. There had been recent rumors that Enrico would be getting engaged to Valentina. What chance did Donetta have at this point? It had taken her a long time to realize that in the end Enrico had stopped loving her. What a stupid, foolish fool she'd been to keep him alive in her heart all this time!

As she'd told him in Madrid a month ago when he'd shown up out of the blue, they'd had their fun living in a dream. But that period when they'd ignored the fact that they were both promised to other people was long since over. Seeing him again had given her the closure she'd needed even if he wasn't wearing a wedding ring yet.

"I find Arnaud very handsome and know he's successful," her mother continued reciting his virtues, breaking into Donetta's tortured thoughts. "We all know how well thought of he is in his country and what a wonderful husband he will make you. Your Zia Ottavia thinks he's perfect for you."

Her aunt's opinion held a lot of sway with her mother.

Suddenly her father sat forward. "It's past time you got married, Donetta." His no-nonsense voice shook as he said it. With his heart condition, Donetta worried when he got this upset. "To think our youngest is already married, yet our oldest is still single. It isn't right. This silliness about you not being ready for marriage has gone too far and has to stop."

"Please consider what we're saying." Her mother got up from the chair and put a hand on her shoulder. "Arnaud will be coming to Domodossola tomorrow. He says it's on business, but we all know the real reason. He's so eager to see you. Will you allow him to call on you tomorrow evening? I'll plan a special dinner."

Her mother never knew when to give up. She took a deep breath. "Do you really like him, Papà?"

He stared at her without blinking. "Of course I do! I've been planning on your marriage for a long time. We've known and liked his parents for many years, too. I'm very impressed with his sincerity. You've had many suitors, but I honestly believe he'll make you a wonderful companion you can love and trust."

Her mother hugged her. "All we ask is that you give him the chance to spend more time with you."

"Amen," her father asserted.

Resigned that her parents weren't going to stop pressuring her, Donetta got up from the table. "Since it's so important to you, go ahead and invite him to dinner, but I can't promise anything."

"I believe something wonderful will come of it," her father reminded her.

She decided to change the subject. "While we're all still here, I wanted to give you some good news. The Carrera charity raised enough funds to pay the work crew's final bill for renovating the Santa Duomo Maria Church that was damaged during the last earthquake. Piero e Figli have done a remarkable job."

"Their work has always been excellent," her mother murmured. "That's my favorite church in the city."

"Mine, too, Mamma. The frescoes are priceless. I just hope more funds keep coming in to start work on some of the other buildings since we can't dip into the treasury."

"Absolutely not." So spoke her father whose voice sounded stronger since her capitulation.

"Then I'll see all of you at dinner tonight."

Fausta shook her head. "I'll be eating in town with Mia."

Her best friend, Mia, a nurse at the Hospital of the Three Crosses, was on Fausta's fund-raising committee. But Fausta was spending more and more time in town with her. Donetta figured there was a compelling reason why she hadn't been around much lately. Fausta continued to meet new men along with Mia, and Donetta had promised to keep it a secret from their parents.

In turmoil over Enrico's disappearance from her life and now her parents' insistence that she marry Arnaud, Donetta gave her parents a kiss and left the dining room.

Dispirited, she headed to the south wing of the fifteenth-century palace, where all the offices were located. She had her own office next to the room where their legislature met. But she was often away from the palace doing fund-raising and goodwill tours.

When she was gone, she relied on her secretary, Talia, to run the daily business, bring in the mail and do odd jobs in her absence. Talia, a married brunette in her thirties with two children, nodded to her as she entered the room.

"You've received something important in the mail this morning. It's stamped top priority and it's from the country of Vallefiore, Your Highness."

CHAPTER TWO

JUST HEARING THE name Vallefiore brought
Donetta close to a faint. Since seeing her last
month, had Enrico decided to write to her
anyway? Why? After his cruel silence over
the years, did he think she'd welcome a letter at this late date?

But her curiosity got the best of her and
her hand trembled as she reached for the envelope. It took a moment before the pounding of her heart calmed down. After sitting in
her swivel chair, she noticed it had been ad-
dressed to Princess Donetta Rossiano of the
Domodossola National Equestrian Association. Donetta had been in charge of it since
she'd stopped performing at twenty-one.

Inside was an official invitation from
Prince Giovanni di Montedoro, head of the
Vallefiore National Equestrian Association.

Not Enrico?

Her heart fell.

Prince Giovanni was always at the *concorsos* with their federation, but until last month she'd never seen Enrico with him since their competitive days. This invitation was announcing an international *concorso* covering the last two days of August, a month from now.

She, along with other invited royals, was to be a special guest of King Nuncio and Queen Teodora, and sit in their box for the events, followed by dinner and a spectacular fireworks presentation by the lake.

Donetta was absolutely amazed. Their country had never sponsored a *concorso* before. Once again her heart pounded unnaturally hard as she took in the information. Entrants from ten to twenty-one years of age would be competing in the capital city of Saracene, the location of the royal palace.

Her thoughts went back to her first competition in England at the age of ten. Donetta had won all the events in her age group on her British thoroughbred, Luna, a young mare her father had purchased for her. Luna's pedigree dated back to Eclipse, the famous race horse from the Windsor Great Park era. How she'd loved that horse and Enrico's!

She'd found out Enrico rode a fabulous Sanfratellano horse from his country, a breed that had existed in some form for centuries. In the Middle Ages the Arabian breed became popular among the Norman nobility, having been preferred by the Saracens who ruled Sicily and other nearby islands like Vallefiore until the eleventh century.

Enrico rode a high-spirited horse from that breed, which in past times could bear the weight of a fully armored knight. In the mountainous islands of the Ionian Sea region, he'd told her, a battle horse's strength was often more important than a lighter horse's speed.

Receiving this invitation from Enrico just after leaving the dining room where her parents had begged her to give Arnaud a chance to settle on an official engagement pained her terribly. Did Enrico want to apologize to her this badly? She didn't get it.

Memories ran through her mind. That day when he'd helped her down from her horse because they'd been riding bareback, he'd pulled her into his arms and kissed her so thoroughly she'd never wanted him to stop.

It had been the thrill of her young life and his image had been burned into her heart and memory. But apparently that moment hadn't meant the same thing to him. Kiss the lovesick girl and sow his wild oats before settling down with Valentina, was that it?

Maybe he'd fallen for someone else he'd met at the university. Or possibly some beauty he'd come across during his travels. Or maybe the answer lay in the simple fact that his youthful, heated feelings for her had abated and he hadn't wanted to take that two-week vacation with her after all.

Donetta would always have questions that would eat her alive if she didn't learn the truth. Maybe she'd get the answers if she attended this *concorso.*

"Talia? Will you please send a message to Prince Giovanni that our equestrian association plans to accept. There's no time like today to start contacting the association staff and participants from around the country to make travel and lodging arrangements."

"Yes, Your Highness."

Donetta's thoughts were running wild. While she was in Vallefiore, she would purchase a Sanfratellano horse for herself and have it shipped home. Besides the king and queen, some of the Montedoro royal family would probably be present at the events. She knew they had two married daughters. Would Enrico also be there to explain his behavior?

He was twenty-seven now. She was surprised he hadn't married Valentina yet. Donetta had always thought he was the most attractive man in the world. No male of her acquaintance ever sat a horse as magnificently. She appreciated beauty in any form.

Before seeing him in Spain she'd lodged some unkind thoughts about him. He'd fallen off the pedestal she'd put him on. But she'd had to scratch her negative thoughts when he'd said he'd come to Spain expressly to see her and apologize.

To make things harder for her, he'd dressed in chinos and a silky brown sports shirt, leaving her breathless. How on earth was she ever going to get him out of her system?

She decided it was a good thing Arnaud would be coming to dinner tomorrow evening to help her deal with what she'd only been able to consider as Enrico's rejection of her.

Her mom was right that Arnaud was handsome in that certain French way. It was long past time she put thoughts of Enrico away for good and accepted the inevitability of marrying Arnaud, who'd been actively pursuing her.

"Talia? I have some shopping to do, but I'll check back with you later." Donetta decided to buy a new dress and shoes. It had been a while.

Apparently her effort didn't go unappreciated. At dinner the next night, Arnaud whispered, "I've never seen you look so *incroyable*. That lovely green dress matches your eyes. I can't stop looking at you, *ma belle*."

"Thank you, Arnaud. You're quite a sight yourself."

He did look pretty amazing in his evening clothes. They wandered out on the terrace off the large dining room after dessert and talked several hours. "You have to know why I'm here. Will you marry me, Donetta?"

She lifted her head. The time for truth had come. "Can you look me in the eye and tell me you're in love with me? You know what I mean. The kind of heart-wrenching love that leaves you breathless and aching inside until nothing else matters in this world?"

He searched her eyes for a long moment before he said, "Why do I get the feeling you've known a love like that?"

She fought not to look away while her guilty heart pounded with sickening speed. "*I* get the feeling you haven't known a love like that yet, or you would have married her without your parents' consent."

The silence convicted both of them.

"Thank you for being honest with me, Arnaud. I do love you for that. Maybe we can make a go of an arranged marriage and children based on a mutual liking and fondness for each other."

"Donetta—"

"Let me finish. I know you like me, and I care for you. But this is the problem of being born to royal parents. They are pressuring you to marry and they've picked me. My parents want me to marry you and have wanted it for a long time. This has been planned and wished for on both sides for years. Though I've liked you better than any of the men who've made proposals, it isn't love."

Up to the point that Enrico's letters had

stopped coming, Donetta had remained resolute in her determination that the two of them had been in love. To her consternation, she feared she'd been deluding herself.

"It can grow into love," Arnaud murmured, breaking into her painful thoughts. "I want you to come to Haute Vienne next weekend. There's so much to show you, and we'll talk. Hopefully you'll fall in love with my home and like me better. Let's find out if we can see our way clear to announce our engagement."

Donetta had to admit she was touched. He *was* sincere and truly a wonderful man. If she broke her own rule and decided to marry since her desire to be queen of Domodossola was hopeless, Arnaud would be the perfect choice for a husband and father of her children. Forget Enrico.

He gripped her hand tighter. "Donetta? Will you come next weekend?"

She closed her eyes. Why not? "Yes, I'll be happy to come. Thank you for inviting me."

"Ma chère," he said in an unsteady voice and pulled her into his arms to kiss her.

She responded to him, waiting for the magic she'd felt when Enrico had hungrily kissed her. But there was no comparison and never could be. She wasn't in love with Arnaud, nor he with her.

Donetta was now a grown woman who'd become somewhat distrustful and cynical after seeing Enrico's picture in the media with other women. She'd also heard rumors of a possible marriage with Valentina.

As for Donetta, she'd been a starry-eyed twenty-one-year-old whose heart had been full of Enrico. But she shouldn't expect to be in that insane condition ever again.

A month later, Enrico rode out early on Friday morning to the Vallefiore National Airport in one limo, Giovanni in another. His staff from the palace were meeting the planes flying in with the contestants and their horses from Domodossola and other countries. They would take them to their lodgings so that Enrico and his cousin were free to meet the royal jet.

He hadn't slept all night in his excitement to see Donetta again. The August *concorso* hadn't come soon enough for him. After installing her at the palace, he wouldn't leave her side during the day's events. Tonight after dinner and fireworks for everyone along the lake's waterfront, he would whisk her away for an overnight campout on the island in his Land Rover.

Enrico had done all the packing and preparations ahead of time. Her associates would take care of Domodossola's participation in the competition, while he enjoyed all day today and tomorrow with her in private.

As the jet taxied to a stop, Giovanni got out of his limo and greeted the two male staff deplaning first. Donetta would be next.

In his official capacity as crown prince, Enrico exited the limo in his white royal summer suit with the blue sash from shoulder to waist. He watched at the bottom of the stairs as she started to descend. But when she saw him, she faltered for an instant before coming all the way.

Between her pale pink three-piece skirt suit and her hair, he was dazzled. Talk about a vision. His hope that she'd come had been realized.

"Donetta? May I be the first to welcome you to my country."

"Thank you, Enrico." She smiled. "I didn't expect to see you again. On behalf of my country, we're happy to be here for this *concorso*."

He reached for her hand to kiss the back of it. "If you'll come with me, we'll drive to the palace, where you can freshen up before the first events in dressage begin at ten a.m."

"My secretary said that my staff and I were booked at the Montedoro Lake Front Hotel."

"I hope you don't mind, but I had you installed at the palace. This is the first time I've been able to show you around. In truth I've wanted this opportunity since I finished my university studies, but my father's poor health changed my world.

"I couldn't tell you about it in my letters because I'd made a promise to my mother to keep silent. She feared word would get out about him. I'm sure it has, but there's been no mention of it in the press yet. She has wanted him protected for as long as possible. Seeing you again, I know I can trust you not to say anything to your staff."

They walked to the limo where the chauffeur helped both of them inside and shut the door. He sat next to her as they drove off.

"I had no idea your father was ill. What's wrong with him?"

He glanced at her lovely profile. "He was diagnosed with Alzheimer's right before my graduation."

"Oh, no—"

"No one except our personal staff knew the truth at the time. Since my return, I've been running the country more and more. Sadly, his condition is now severe."

A small gasp escaped her throat. "Is he bedridden?"

"No. His caregiver gets him dressed and sees that he's fed. Mostly he sits in a wheelchair near Mamma. He has a total lack of awareness and can't take care of his daily activities. Besides agitation, he occasionally has a hallucination and even wanders at times. His paranoia is worse and he doesn't know the family."

Donetta turned to him. "How horrible. I'm so sorry, Enrico."

Her sincerity tugged on his emotions. "My mother and sisters can hardly bear it. He's Mamma's whole life."

"So she's been totally dependent on you since you came home?"

He nodded.

Donetta bowed her head. "The people in

my country don't know about my father's heart trouble, either. Our family is worried about him, but at least he knows us and still has help from Stefano in running things. How do you handle it?"

"A day at a time. After seeing you in Madrid, I talked it over with my cousin Giovanni to host a *concorso* here. I'd hoped you'd come so I could explain certain things to you. I've needed to take a few days off for some real enjoyment."

She smoothed her suit skirt. "I'll admit I was surprised when my office received your invitation."

"I, for one, am very glad you decided to accept it. When we were younger, you asked me a lot of questions about the Sanfratellano horses. I thought I'd take you to some places where they run wild and you can see them for yourself."

"I'd love it!" She'd said it without hesitation.

"After this evening's fireworks we'll drive to that part of the island and camp out so you can watch them at first light."

"In tents?" He felt her excitement, which was contagious.

"Or in sleeping bags under the stars. I'll bring food for us. What do you think?"

"You've made it impossible for me to turn you down."

That was the idea.

Donetta's eyes widened as they came in sight of the fabulous Montedoro palace, which was reflective of the Mudejar and Renaissance décors of former times. An enchanting garden and pools lined in beautiful *azulejos* tiles took her breath away. The Moors and Romans had left traces of their cultures behind.

Enrico accompanied her up the steps into the south wing and walked her to her apartment on the second floor, where her luggage had been placed. He left her at the door. "There's a tray of food for you if you're hungry. I'll be back for you in twenty minutes and we'll leave for the stand at the exhibition grounds."

"Thank you, Enrico."

When he left, she rested against the closed door, trying to get a grip on her emotions. Hearing some of the details of his life since college had told her how wrong she'd been in her thinking about him, and it had left her shaken.

She looked up at the intricate fretwork ceiling reminiscent of those at the Alhambra in Spain, where she'd been recently. Awestruck by such beauty, she wandered over to the arched Moorish windows that overlooked a pool in the inner courtyard. This was Enrico's home.

Seeing such a gorgeous man standing at the foot of the stairs outside her plane a little while ago, dressed in royal whites, had almost given her a heart attack. When she'd decided to come to Vallefiore, she hadn't been sure she would even see him.

From the moment she'd caught sight of his black hair and tall, fit physique, nothing had unfolded the way she'd imagined. For one thing, she'd learned he was acting king now. All the power and authority rested on his shoulders, but if anyone could handle it, he could.

To think he'd spent the last five years supporting his father and family at a time of great sorrow for all of them had changed her thinking.

Confused and conflicted by some of her

earlier negative thoughts about him not being sincere, she freshened up and then walked into the Moorish-inspired sitting room to eat. There was juice, coffee, mint tea, rolls and pastries, sugared almonds, anything you could want.

Enrico had gone all out for her. Why would he do this now and stage a *concorso* to see her? Did he think she was so angry that only an invitation like this could bring her here? But to go to so much trouble didn't make sense. In truth, she didn't understand his motives.

A knock on the outer door caused her to jump. She finished her last bite of roll, reached for her purse and hurried to let him in.

His black eyes played over her in the same way they'd done before, when they'd stayed in the rental car, wanting to hold on to each other the night before having to say goodbye. It had sent heat through her body then, too. "Are you ready, or do you need more time?"

Donetta couldn't get over how devastatingly attractive he was. It was hard to breathe. "I'd like to go so we won't be late for the entrants in the ten-year-olds' division. I'll never forget my first performance and how nervous I was."

"I watched your outstanding performance and would never have guessed you had a nervous bone in your body."

"A lot you know." His flattery was getting to her.

He helped her down the magnificent staircase to the doors of the south entrance. The bright sun was warming the air by the second as they walked to the limo and climbed in. After a short ride they came to a huge park.

A canopied stand filled with invited spectators from the royal family had been erected midway to another canopy where tables with tablecloths and flower centerpieces had been set up for lunch.

Once the limo stopped, Enrico escorted her up the few steps to the dais reserved for the royal family. In one glance Donetta saw that he had a stunning brunette mother and brunette sisters who sat with their husbands. Naturally, his father was missing.

Enrico cupped her elbow. "Donetta? May I present my mother, Queen Teodora?"

"Your Majesty." Donetta curtsied to her.

"Mamma. Please meet Princess Donetta Rossiano of Domodossola."

His mother put out a hand to shake Donetta's. "I'm pleased to meet you, my dear. I've heard you're a great equestrian and a beauty. Now at least I can see you live up to your reputation for the latter."

But there was frost in her voice. Something was definitely wrong. Was she incensed that Donetta, from an enemy country, had been invited and had come to the *concorso* when the queen was expecting her son to marry Valentina?

Donetta smiled into his mother's dark brown eyes, but the queen didn't smile back. With that last comment, Donetta had got the feeling his mother was in shock. It went beyond the natural aversion from the queen over the feud that had separated their two countries for so many years.

"Thank you. I want you to know I'm the one who's honored to meet you, Your Majesty. My parents have asked me to convey their greetings to you and King Nuncio. I'm sorry to hear he isn't feeling well today."

The queen ignored Donetta's comment.

"We hope to host the first of many *concorsos* in the future."

"Mamma?" Enrico interjected. Obviously he'd noticed his mother's deliberate snub. "If you'll excuse us, I want Donetta to meet Lia and Catarina and their husbands."

"The performance is about to start, Enrico."

Donetta got the impression he'd infuriated his mother.

"There's still time."

He cupped Donetta's elbow and introduced her to his sisters, one of whom was pregnant, and their husbands. The four of them were gracious and smiled, making her feel better. Then he helped her take her place next to him while he sat by the queen.

His cousin Prince Giovanni took over the microphone to announce the opening of the *concorso*, and the competition began.

Watching the young entrants for the next two hours took Donetta back in time. But as each age division performed, she realized no participant displayed Enrico's outstanding horsemanship. Year after year, he'd been the master she'd hero-worshipped.

But leaving for university had prevented

him from entering any more horse competitions for his country. Once Donetta had finished college, her father had asked her to run their country's horse federation.

When there was a break in events, Enrico leaned closer. "Your country's participants are exceptional, but no one rides the way you did," he said in a low voice.

"I was thinking the same thing about you."

"That's nice to hear. Walk with me to the other canopy, where we'll be served lunch before the jumping competitions start. If you need to freshen up, there are restrooms behind the canopy."

"That's good to know, but I'm fine right now, thank you."

Everyone in the stand followed them to the tables. Donetta expected Enrico to help his mother, but she noticed one of her sons-in-law had already started to escort the queen. Donetta was being given special treatment and knew his mother had to be close to apoplectic that she'd dared come to Vallefiore.

Once Enrico had helped her to sit at an individual table and took a chair opposite her, she couldn't stay silent any longer. "Enrico? When there are officials from other countries represented here, why are you showing me this exceptional kind of interest? Your attention to me is like a slap in the face to your mother."

She had to wait for his answer because the palace staff had already started to serve them lunch and iced tea before they could have privacy. There was only a certain amount of time to eat in order to stay with the day's agenda.

"Because years ago you and I were attracted to each other and planned to take a vacation together. Unfortunately that didn't work out. But you have to know I've always wanted you to be my guest. To my chagrin, life happened when I had other plans. Up to now, problems have been the story of my life." His frank speaking melted her heart.

No one knew that better than Donetta, whose royal responsibilities were forcing her to consider marriage to Arnaud. Her last visit to Haute Vienne hadn't helped her make up her mind. She still hadn't been able to tell him she'd marry him. But she'd promised that after this trip to Vallefiore, she would give him an answer one way or the other.

Enrico's dark eyes bored into hers, sending

a thrill through her body. "The damn fraud case that caused our two countries to cease all business was never proven and should have ended years ago. Under my reign I intend to have it investigated and solve the mystery so I can reopen negotiations with your father."

Was the feud the reason he'd cut off relations with her? "That would be so wonderful, Enrico."

"I agree. Even more important, it's a miracle you're here at all. I couldn't have been more excited when Giovanni told me you had accepted our invitation."

Everything he was saying to her now had resurrected her old feelings of desire for him while she enjoyed the exquisite seafood salad. "I have to admit I was excited to come to the country that produced your magnificent horse Rajah and hopefully see you again in your own surroundings. We used to talk a lot about each other's lives."

"Being with you was always the highlight of my trips to those competitions," he confessed.

She had to suppress a moan. "I felt the same way." Clearly, they'd both been crazy about each other despite knowing it was wrong, but destiny had kept them apart.

"Donetta?" His voice broke in on her tumultuous thoughts. "It's time to go back to the stand. Are you ready?"

"I am. The lunch was delicious. Thank you." She stood up and followed him over to their seats behind Giovanni, who was ready to announce the afternoon's activities. All the while she felt the queen's hostile brown gaze on her.

The jumping trials were her favorite discipline to watch, but her mind was so full of Enrico and their conversation she had a hard time concentrating. At the end of the day Giovanni made the announcement that the crown prince himself would give out the awards.

Donetta's gaze stayed glued on the gorgeous acting king as he stood before the awestruck winners and honored each of them with their cups. One young man from Domodossola won a first place in the sixteen-year-olds' division. Though she was excited for him, it was Enrico who filled her vision.

Her heart thudded when she realized she wouldn't be flying back home until tomorrow evening. For once she didn't have to say goodbye to Enrico. He'd planned for them to spend the night and next day together.

In the past she'd always walked to the stables to talk to her country's participants and see their horses firsthand, but not today. Enrico wanted to get going and not waste time.

Luckily, Donetta always brought several changes of casual outfits. Since Enrico was taking her camping, she had a choice of pants and blouses to wear and decided on her tan pants and hunter green blouse.

After talking to Giovanni and congratulating him on supervising such an outstanding *concorso*, Donetta climbed into the limo with Enrico and they were driven back to the palace, where she could change out of her suit.

He walked her to the door of her suite. "I'll come by for you in an hour. Does that give you enough time?"

"An hour is perfect. Enrico?"

"Yes?"

"Before you go, I just wanted to say that because you're the crown prince, you gave all of today's winners a great thrill presenting them with their cups. That one young girl from Spain looked so excited to meet you she reminded me of myself when Queen Anne handed me my trophy. This day will stand out in all their minds."

His black eyes gleamed, leaving her breathless. "As long as it has been memorable for you, that's all I ask."

The second he left, she closed the door and removed her pink suit, but her body was trembling. She took a shower and washed her hair. It didn't take long to dry and style.

Ten minutes later Donetta heard the knock on the door. She gathered her suitcase and purse and hurried to open it, coming face-to-face with Enrico. He had to be the most dashing male on the planet. She swallowed hard as she took in his rock-solid physique.

No longer in his whites, he wore khaki pants and a matching short-sleeved khaki shirt open at the neck. His black eyes and hair, combined with such a burnished complexion, made her joints go weak.

She felt his eyes wander over her, causing her pulse to race. "You should always wear green," he said in his deep voice. "Have you forgotten anything? We won't be coming back until tomorrow. I hope you won't mind that we miss dinner and the fireworks.

I have other plans for us." Her pulse flew off the charts. "Does your pilot know you won't be flying home until late in the day?"

"I'll let him know. Enrico? What about your mother? Is she aware you're with me tonight? I didn't come to Vallefiore to cause more discord between our two countries."

"I have no doubts she knows what we're doing. She has her spies. If I'm not wrong, she's supervising the help putting my father to bed and complaining to him about any number of things she can't change. She believes he understands, even if he doesn't talk. Sadly, I don't think he does, but it helps her to let off steam."

Donetta moaned. "She must be upset that you're entertaining a Rossiano."

"Could be, but I don't care."

Neither did she. Being with him like this tonight was all she could think about.

CHAPTER THREE

Enrico helped Donetta into the Land Rover. Surrounded by heavy security, he drove them toward the mountains in the distance. They still had two hours of daylight left. Time for her to take in the scenery while he set up camp for them.

It wasn't long before she exclaimed, "The landscape is so green and fertile! Do you get a lot more rain here than I had supposed?"

He chuckled. "I'm glad you've noticed. It means my work since returning from England hasn't been in vain."

"What do you mean?"

"It's not rain but irrigation. Let me explain. Since agriculture forms the basis of Vallefiore's economy, Giovanni and I have studied the agricultural challenges of our country. Between us we developed a system of piping and pumps to cover the huge island with fresh water converted from sea water.

"This innovation has brought whole new possibilities for more jobs for our young people, more money for infrastructure, increased production of our pipe manufacturing plants as well as a profusion of farm implements.

"Our farmers are growing three times as much produce, which means enriching the economy and exports. We're building timber assets now in demand internationally and contributing to the country's prosperity."

"I'm so impressed I don't know where to start."

Enrico chuckled. "Even though there's much work to be done yet, we're satisfied about the progress made so far. But the agricultural problems are only part of my responsibilities and worries. My other important work stretches further to oversee national security in order to establish law and order. We have a lot of problems right now."

"What kind?"

"Well, I've stopped the construction of most new renewable energy projects. I'm trying to ensure that the corruptive elements of society are rooted out of the industry before allowing fresh projects to go forward.

"Though my father has worked on the problem, he hadn't been aggressive enough. I've seen that their influence in the country has to be wiped out by vetting those businesses affected and jailing the heads, no matter the consequences. Between that and our water needs, I've been busy."

Her eyes widened. "You've managed to put in pipelines all over this huge island to pump in the sea water and make it potable?"

Enrico nodded. "We've a long way to go to cover the whole island, but in the last three years we've seen some success and are encouraged by what is happening."

Her smile lit up a spot inside him he didn't know was there. "It's a miracle what you've done so far. I can't tell you how in awe I am."

"Enough to forgive me for ending the letter writing? I didn't mean for it to be permanent, but when I reached home, between the concerns of the government and the needs of my mother, I barely had time to put one foot in front of the other."

"Of course I forgive you."

"Then you're a saint."

"Hardly. Look what you've done for your country so far! To think what could be done for some of the countries of East Africa suffering from drought."

"I think about it all the time."

Talking to Donetta had always stimulated him, but never more than now. While they were talking, he'd driven them into the mountains. "Before dark there's a sight I want you to see. It's around this next curve." A minute later he pulled his Land Rover to the side of the road.

When a cry escaped her lips, it was the most satisfying sound he'd heard in a long time. With the sun getting ready to set, its last reflection was captured by the spectacular waterfall, the longest one on the island.

"The locals call it Percorso al Cielo."

"The pathway to heaven," she murmured. "How absolutely beautiful."

He glanced at her. "When I first saw you perform on your horse, the hair cascading a silvery gold almost to your waist beneath your helmet reminded me of this waterfall. When I saw you last month, I was surprised to see you looked a lot different from my boyhood memory of you."

She turned to him. "Do you know your hair was one of the first things I noticed about you when you were just ten?"

He smiled. "I hope to keep it for a while."

"I can't imagine you losing it."

"That day will come."

"Maybe when you're eighty."

"I like your vote of confidence." They laughed as he drove back on the road.

"Where are we going?"

"To our campsite to eat and get ready for bed. It's about ten minutes from here, on a bluff that overlooks part of the plain."

"I can't wait to see the wild horses."

"When you've had your fill tomorrow, we'll come back and swim in the pool beneath the waterfall."

Her eyes met his. "That sounds like heaven, but I didn't bring a swimming suit."

"No problem. We keep spares at the palace for visitors. I brought one for you in my knapsack."

Before long they reached the bluff. He found a spot beyond the trees to park the car next to the pit he'd dug years ago and always used when he cooked out. "Do you want me to set up a tent tonight?"

"Oh, no. It's a warm evening and I love sleeping out in the open." Donetta was a woman after his own heart, which was pounding unhealthily fast. "Let me help you."

She opened the door of the Land Rover and walked around to the rear to get the sleeping bags. They worked in harmony. Enrico set up a small camping table and chairs, aware the bodyguards were somewhere around. Then he got out a cooler along with his flashlight and a liter of water.

While she made coffee and cut the bread to make fried bruschetta with the ingredients he'd brought, Enrico got a fire going and put down the grill to cook their steaks, potatoes and the bread for the bruschetta. Soon they sat on the chairs to eat their food with the greatest enjoyment. Enrico hadn't had this much fun in his whole life.

He slanted her a glance. "How did you learn to be such an excellent cook?"

"The palace chef took my sisters and me under her wing. She once said, 'Princess or pauper, you need to learn how to prepare food. You never know when it will come in handy.' When I get back to the palace I'm going to thank her for all those lessons."

"I'll send her my own letter," he declared. "I've never eaten fried bruschetta. It's ambrosia and I don't ever want to eat it any other way."

She smiled at him in the firelight, which brought out her classic features and the high cheekbones that emphasized her beauty. "I think it tastes so good because we're out of doors. I'm sure I've told you before that my sisters and I loved to play in the woods outside the palace. Occasionally we'd rescue a creature like a wounded bird. My sister Fausta was good at giving first aid and nursed several rabbits back to health.

"Do you know when my sister Lanza was on her honeymoon, they found a little red fox in the snow? They took care of it and she wanted to keep it, but in the end they put it in a wildlife shelter."

Enrico ate the last of the bruschetta. "Sounds like you and your sisters had a lot of fun growing up. My sisters and I did, too."

"I remember some of the antics you told me about in your letters."

"Giovanni often joined us. We hiked a lot and played in the lake in front of the palace.

Some nights we slept out on the sand so we could fish from our sleeping bags."

She chuckled. "What fun! Luckily for your sisters, you were there to protect them, so your parents probably weren't alarmed. But Papà worried about us and wouldn't let us stay outside at night. If I could have, I would have built my own secret hideout deep in the forest by the lake and slept in it every night. I should have been born a boy."

Laughter burst out of Enrico. Everything she said enamored him. "I can't picture it."

"Boys have a lot more fun and can do everything."

"So can girls."

"Not when you're royal and born in my country."

Their conversation had taken a sudden turn that brought veracity to Giovanni's inside information about her ambition to rule on her own. Translating what she'd said, he understood that Donetta couldn't grow up to be queen.

Enrico got to his feet to start the cleanup. He'd let the fire die down until it was time to go to sleep. "Your father let you become one of the finest equestrians in your country. As

I recall, he bought you your first horse that came from a champion."

She nodded. "You're right about that and I love him for it."

"Just think. Without him, we would never have met."

They stared at each other for an overly long moment. "I'm sure that's true." In the next breath Donetta did her part to help him. After he suggested she go behind one of the trees for privacy, he laid out their sleeping bags with pillows side by side, adding an extra blanket for her if she wanted it.

Once he'd locked up the food and cooler in the car, he doused the embers and waited in his bag for her return. He would sleep in his clothes and put on a fresh outfit in the morning.

It looked like she'd decided to do the same thing as she walked toward him. The three-quarter moon had just come up over the mountain and the light illuminated her hair.

"Your bed is waiting for you."

Donetta laughed gently and climbed inside. "This has been a magical day, Enrico."

"It should have happened after I got back from England. A lot of life has gone on in the meantime." He turned toward her, rising up on one elbow. "Donetta—what's happened to your understanding with Arnaud? I'm asking because if it is still on and I were he, I'd be ripped apart with jealousy."

She lay on her back, staring up into the heavens. "We were together recently. He's asked me to marry him, but I haven't given him an answer yet."

"Does he know about our past?"

"No."

"Are you going to tell him?"

"I'll have to if I decide to accept his proposal."

Such stark honesty caused Enrico to suck in his breath. "Why did you agree to come camping with me?"

She turned on her side toward him. "Why do you think? Though your invitation here has come years too late for my liking, I couldn't resist accepting, if only to find out if I'd been harboring a false memory."

"In what way false?"

He heard a troubled sigh escape. "Had I been foolish to think you'd cared for me all those years?"

The high-pitched sound of a jackdaw rent the air. "You *know* I cared."

"But we didn't go away on that vacation. I understand why, but it has been a long time. Too long," she whispered.

Her mournful response resonated in his heart. Suddenly she rolled on her side away from him before he could reach out to kiss her. She needed convincing.

"Tomorrow I'll waken you early to see a sight you'll never forget. *Buona notte*, Donetta."

"*Dormi bene*, Enrico."

Sleep well? Between his desire for her and the need to protect her even with the security hidden beyond the trees, he doubted he'd sleep at all. But to his surprise he did succumb at last and didn't stir until his watch alarm went off at six thirty.

He looked over at Donetta, who was still sound asleep. Taking care to be quiet, he got out of his bag and freshened up before preparing coffee for them. In the cooler were ham-filled rolls and plums to serve for breakfast. For snacks he'd brought his favorite sugared almonds.

With everything ready, he walked over to

her sleeping bag and hunkered down. The sun was just coming up over the mountains. "Donetta?" He gave her a little nudge and she rolled over. When she opened those fabulous green eyes of hers, he got lost in them. "Good morning. It's time to get up."

"*Buon giorno.* I can't believe I slept so well. I hope *you* did."

He nodded. "It has to be this air."

"I agree. It's heavenly here. Excuse me for a minute while I freshen up."

She got out of her bag and slid on her sandals, then hurried behind the trees for privacy. When she reappeared, she looked good enough to eat with that glorious hair slightly disheveled and no makeup, which she didn't need anyway. He motioned her over to the camp table, where he handed her a mug of coffee.

"Umm. You've even fixed breakfast for us. You'll make someone a marvelous wife one day," she teased before sitting down to eat.

Amused, Enrico walked over to the car and brought back a pair of binoculars that he put on the table. "These are extra powerful and will come in handy for you."

"Thanks. You've thought of everything.

I'll never be able to repay you for all you've done."

He was pleased to see she was hungry and ate everything. "I've been waiting for this a long time. Your being here is payment enough. When the invitation for the competition went out, I'd hoped your country would accept, but I wasn't at all sure that *you* would come as well."

"I told the queen it was an honor for us. I wouldn't have missed it."

As he bit into another roll, they felt vibrations beneath their feet. "The horses are coming. Quick, Donetta. Follow me to the blanket I spread out. We'll lie on it to watch."

In another half minute they lay side by side on their stomachs. He handed her the binoculars. The thundering grew louder, and suddenly, the plain below was filled with black, brown and bay horses galloping for what Enrico believed was the sheer joy of being alive.

"Oh—" Donetta cried out in awe. "Look how gorgeous they are! It's unbelievable."

He knew exactly how she felt to see such majesty loose and free in the wilds. "I marvel every time."

The herd followed their leader, a magnificent black stallion. "Look how he changes directions and they all keep up with him. They're having their own kind of fun, aren't they?"

"They do it for hours."

"Who says horses don't enjoy themselves."

"I think they probably have more fun than some people do," he concurred. Donetta had his same kind of love for horses and saw what he saw, bonding them in a unique way.

She studied them through the binoculars for a long time. "The leader looks like Rajah!"

"They're all from the same bloodline."

Another hour passed while they shared the binoculars and she let out sigh after sigh. "They're all so beautiful."

"Have you decided you have a favorite color?"

"Yes. The ones with satin coats that look like melted dark chocolate in the sun. They're sleek and breathtaking, don't you think?" She suddenly turned to look at him. Their faces were only inches apart.

"Almost as breathtaking as you." Without worrying about the bodyguards, he put his arm around her shoulders and pulled her to him. Her mouth was even more luscious than he'd remembered. He wanted her more than any woman he'd ever been with in his life.

"Enrico—"

The way she said his name and kissed him back told him she'd been hungering for this, too. Unable to stop, he crushed her to him and began to devour her in earnest.

No longer aware of their surroundings, they were on fire for each other. They lost track of time, trying to assuage their needs. He was on the verge of telling her he was in love with her when the ringing of her phone penetrated the silence.

"Oh, no—"

Donetta groaned and pulled out of his arms. "I forgot to phone Arnaud and let him know when I'd be back." She struggled to her feet and hurried over to her sleeping bag to get it.

Enrico stayed put to give her privacy while he looked out over the plain. By now the horses had disappeared for the day, along with a moment he would treasure forever. But that moment wouldn't be the last because more than ever Enrico was determined to marry her and intended to carry out his original plan before she left Vallefiore.

Donetta grabbed her phone. Seeing Arnaud's name on the caller ID filled her with fresh guilt. She was shaking so much she sank down on her sleeping bag so she wouldn't fall. She'd promised to phone him but had forgotten.

Watching the wild horses running in the early morning had been a breathtaking moment with Enrico that she would never forget. Right now, she was so confused that she couldn't face talking to Arnaud. She would have to call him later.

The second she made that decision, she phoned the pilot and the plan was made for her and her group to fly home at four thirty. With that done, she clicked off and noticed Enrico had packed everything in the Land Rover but her sleeping bag.

She got to her feet and carried it and the pillow to the car. He put it in the back while she climbed in the front seat. Her watch said twelve thirty—too late to make other plans for the day.

"Are you ready for a swim in the pool beneath the waterfall?"

Donetta shook her head. "I'd love to, but after talking to the pilot, I don't think we have the time." She didn't dare be alone with Enrico or she'd never want to go home. "When we get back to the palace, I need to contact my staff and make certain everyone is on the other plane by four thirty."

"I'll admit I'm disappointed, but I understand." He started the car and they left for the city. "Because of time constraints, we'll stop at the village we passed at the base of the mountains and eat lunch. There's a café with the best *crocchè* and *involtini di pesca spada* you've ever tasted. But if you don't care for swordfish, they serve stuffed sardines with pine nuts that are delicious."

"It all sounds wonderful. This whole outing has been out of this world."

Before coming to Vallefiore, Donetta had planned on buying a horse from Enrico's country. That was impossible now. To get any more involved with Enrico would be a grave mistake on every level. He hadn't told her he loved her, let alone asked her to marry him. She'd hoped, prayed it would happen.

But since those words had never passed his lips, this had to be the last time she would ever see him.

"Donetta? Why did you honestly come to Vallefiore?"

"Because you were my teenage crush I never got over. Our relationship has been like reading a book I never finished and never knew how it ended until this morning when you kissed me and I kissed you back.

"I'm not sorry for sleeping out with you and kissing you. I wanted it. But we both know that book is now closed, never to be opened again."

She now knew why he'd gotten her to fly here. He'd wanted to explain why their relationship hadn't been able to work out. Now it was her turn to explain something to him. "I plan to be Arnaud's wife soon and he has to know I will always be faithful to him."

"You'll marry him even though you're not in love with him?"

His honesty took her aback. "I never said that."

"You didn't have to."

Enrico didn't mince words. He'd apologized

for what had gone wrong years ago, but he wasn't in love with her.

Donetta cleared her throat. "I'm hoping love will come and hopefully children."

"What about pleasing yourself?" Donetta didn't expect that question and started to feel uncomfortable. "If you could have your heart's desire, what would it be?"

She stifled a moan. "I've given up on that dream."

"You had a dream?"

"Don't ask. It no longer matters."

Donetta had made two fatal mistakes. Both were the result of losing sight of her goal to be queen in her own right and never taking a husband. But that logic had been fatally flawed from the beginning since it had ruled out children. Just now, when she'd mentioned them in the context of having a family, she knew she wanted children more than anything.

Looking back, she saw that her reason for coming to Vallefiore had been wrong because she'd been hurt by her perception of Enrico's rejection and had wanted answers as to why he didn't love her. Though he'd told her he'd been busy taking on the burdens of his father, if he'd truly loved her, she was convinced he would have found a way to see her long before now.

He'd always taken first place in every international competition from ten to eighteen. After lying in his arms this morning as his kisses brought her rapture, she realized he still held that place in her heart. But he couldn't tell her he was in love with her. It just wasn't meant to be.

If she didn't marry Arnaud, she knew she'd stay single for the rest of her life. That meant she'd never have children. One thing she did know was this: if nothing else, children would bring both her and Arnaud happiness.

The time would come when Arnaud would be king of Haute Vienne, with Donetta at his side. By tomorrow night, both sets of parents would be overjoyed to find out she and Arnaud had made official plans to marry, particularly when her father was ill. He wanted to see her settled.

You're going to get your wish, Papà.

CHAPTER FOUR

DONETTA WAS SO deep in thought she didn't realize that Enrico had turned into the parking area of a charming café.

"You've been so quiet. I hope everything's all right," he said as he helped her out of the car.

"I'm fine, thank you."

They ate lunch on the terrace with its many flowering pots and trees. Clients and waiters alike recognized the crown prince, but they kept their distance with his security men keeping watch. That didn't prevent every woman in sight from staring at him with longing in their eyes, wishing they were with him instead of Donetta.

Once they'd finished their delicious meal, he helped her back into the Land Rover and they continued on to the palace in Saracene.

He drove them to the entrance and helped her to the suite with her suitcase.

"I have to go, but I'll be back in fifteen minutes to take you to the airport." He was out the door in an instant.

This was goodbye. Somehow she had to pull herself together and get ready for the flight. After a quick shower, she dressed in her pink suit and did her makeup in record time.

Too soon she heard the knock on the door. She grabbed her purse and suitcase before answering it. Enrico had also changed and stood there in a tan summer suit with a white shirt open at the neck. No man in this world looked as marvelous as he did.

"Let's go." He reached for her suitcase and they left the palace for the limo parked outside the steps. They sat opposite each other en route to the airport.

"While we're alone, there's something I'd like to talk to you about."

"Of course." She dreaded leaving him and couldn't imagine what was on his mind.

"This is just between us. The fact is, I too am hoping to get married in the near future."

She'd never been so shocked in her life, or

in so much pain. So there *had* been another woman! But Donetta couldn't be upset with him for kissing her when she'd willingly succumbed to him.

Donetta kneaded her hands, not able to look at him. "Only hoping?"

"This princess isn't free to marry me."

Her head reared. "Why not?"

"Because she's supposed to marry another man. But I happen to know she's not in love with him."

What? "Does she know you want to marry her?"

"No."

"Why not?"

"What I have to ask of her will demand a lot since our marriage will be in name only."

Donetta was aghast. "That's no marriage, Enrico. You're not making sense."

He leaned forward. "I need a queen who'll be willing to rule while I do my own work. I believe the princess I want will feel the same way I do and is capable of fulfilling that role."

She was so stunned by his remark she had trouble forming words. "But being the ruler is *your* work. I don't understand what you mean."

"I want a companion who can handle being queen."

"But she *will* be when you marry her. My mother has been a great help to my father and I'm sure yours has been there for your father, too."

Enrico shook his head. "It's not the same thing. I expect her to reign equally with me so I can be left to do my work getting rid of the corruption while she runs the ordinary business of the kingdom."

Donetta stirred restlessly because her heart was thudding too hard for her to remain still. "Will the laws of your country allow such a thing?"

"They will if I'm the king. On my wedding day I'll be crowned and my word will be law."

She was astounded. "Have you discussed this with your mother? How does she feel about this?"

"You already know the answer to that. Valentina and I were promised to each other years ago by our families. But I'm not in love with her, and for all her sweetness, Valentina isn't up to the job of managing the kingdom at this delicate time. Since I know she has feelings for me, I don't want to hurt her."

"Your mother will be crushed, Enrico."

"You're right. Fortunately, the woman I want to marry would be able to deal with the grief my mother will give her. I'm afraid Mamma has very strict attitudes about everything and won't approve. She believes the place of the king's bride is at his side, in a wifely capacity."

No one could relate better than Donetta to the hurt and offense caused by what some might say was a sexist remark. "She's not alone in her thinking, Enrico. My own mother feels the same way."

"That's why I wanted to talk to you about this. No one would have more insight than you. The truth is, I never wanted to be king, but we don't always get what we want in this life and I've had to accept it as my lot."

Donetta had no idea he'd felt that way. The subject hadn't come up during their many conversations or in their letter writing. "Never?"

He shook his head.

"You remind me of my brother-in-law, Stefano. He didn't want the royal life, either. For ten years he was exempted by official decree, until his brother died. At that point Alberto had been engaged to my sister Lanza. In the end Stefano married her, but he had to be re-instated as crown prince first."

"He must have loved your sister a great deal to be willing to become royal again."

"Not in the beginning, but their marriage has turned into a loving one."

"Then that should give you hope that your marriage to Arnaud will turn into a loving one, too, Donetta."

"I'm going to try," she whispered, but she was shaken after being taken into his confidence like this.

"Do you have advice for me on how to reach out to her before it's too late? You and I have always been friends. More important, you're the one person I feel the most comfortable with talking about this. Anything you could say would—"

But before he could finish, *his* phone broke the silence. A frown marred his features after he pulled it out of his shirt pocket and checked the caller ID.

"What's wrong? Is it your father?"

"No, but I have to get back to the palace."

By now they'd reached the part of the airport reserved for private planes. The limo drew up to the royal jet from Domodossola. Giovanni had already arrived with her staff, who were boarding.

The limo driver opened the door for them. Enrico helped her out and walked her to the bottom step. "I'm afraid it's too late to continue our talk."

She still hadn't gotten over the shock. "Will you tell me something first?"

He eyed her through narrowed lids. "Ask me anything."

"Is she a princess I may have met and known? It could make a difference in what I tell you. But if you don't feel comfortable, I totally understand."

His black gaze impaled her. "I thought you knew exactly."

Donetta put a hand to her throat. "But how could I?"

"Maybe this will help. Her royal name is Louisa Regina Donetta Rossiano."

Giovanni sat across from Enrico, eyeing him with avid curiosity. "Out with it, cousin. I want to know one thing. Was the *concorso* a winner? You know what I mean."

Enrico rested his head against the back

of the seat. "It was, until I found out she's planning to marry Arnaud. The gossip you heard about her never planning to marry was wrong."

"Then something has changed," Giovanni exclaimed. "You weren't there when Mia conveyed that info to me."

"Arnaud found a way to break through, because she's going to accept his proposal."

"I'm sorry, cousin. Your mother called me after the competition last evening and wanted to know what I knew about you and Princess Donetta. She was livid over the attention you were giving her. I told her Donetta was simply a guest, but when she found out you'd left the city with her in the Land Rover, she was visibly upset."

"She would be," Enrico muttered.

"When is Donetta's wedding?"

"They haven't planned anything yet."

Giovanni whistled.

"I had to spring my plan on her at the last minute."

"How did that turn out?"

"It didn't."

"Don't be cryptic. I want details," Giovanni pressed.

For the rest of the drive, Enrico filled him in. "She admitted she'd once had a crush on me, but Donetta is an honorable woman who's now planning marriage."

"It goes against everything I heard about her from Mia."

"You're right. It appears that somewhere along the way she abandoned her dream to stay single."

"Well, it would make sense when she's not going to be able to change the law to be queen."

"I should have gone after her when college was over."

"But your hands were full taking over for your father and implementing all the plans for the kingdom. It was a rough time to plan a marriage knowing how your mother felt."

"None of that matters now. I've got to put her out of my mind."

"Good luck on that." Giovanni shook his head. "With the king so much worse, I'm afraid Zia Teodora will be pushing you to marry Valentina."

"It's not going to happen. Unless I meet a woman who could matter to me more than Donetta, I have no plans for marriage."

"Enrico—"

"Like I said, I waited too long to propose to her. As for your help, I haven't thanked you for all you did to make the *concorso* a huge success. I know how hard you've worked and I'm indebted to you for being my friend all my life. Promise you won't leave when you get married."

"Do you know something I don't?"

Enrico looked out at the lake. Its light green color would be the constant reminder of Donetta's incredible eyes. This morning he'd held her in his arms. Her breathtaking response as a prelude before he made love to her for the first time had transformed him. He'd never be the same.

"I can guarantee you'll be married long before I ever consider it."

By some miracle Donetta made it up the steps inside the jet without fainting. For the ninety-minute flight to Domodossola, she sat there trembling, not speaking to anyone. Thank heaven she wouldn't be seeing Arnaud tonight. She needed time to process everything Enrico had just told her.

No sooner had Donetta entered the palace through her private entrance and gone to her bedroom on the second floor than Fausta knocked on the door.

"Donetta?"

She couldn't wipe the tears from her face fast enough. "Come in."

Her sister took one look at her and sat down on the bed beside her. "I *knew* something was wrong when you came flying past my room. I thought you were out with Arnaud."

Donetta got up to get some tissues from the end table. "He's taking me for dinner tomorrow evening."

"Did you have an argument? Is that why you're crying?"

"Oh, Fausta, I'm crying for so many reasons I don't know where to begin."

"I've never seen you this fragmented in my life. Something tells me this is about your visit to Vallefiore. You saw Enrico, of course."

There was no hiding anything from her sister. "Yes."

Fausta got up from the bed and walked over to her. "Do you wish you hadn't gone?"

More tears trickled down Donetta's hot cheeks. "No."

"I see. Is he as gorgeous as I remember?"

She sucked in her breath. "He's so much more that I don't have words."

"He would be," Fausta theorized. "What is he now? Twenty-six? Seven?"

Donetta nodded.

"Did he take you riding?"

The question was a natural one considering their history. She sniffed. "Oddly enough, we didn't have time to do that."

"So what *did* you do?"

She stared at her sister. "After the competition, Enrico took me camping in the mountains. We cooked dinner over a fire and I made him fried bruschetta, which he devoured."

"Ehi—"

"Last night we slept out under the stars in sleeping bags. Early this morning he wakened me so we could watch wild horses run across the plain. The ground thundered beneath us. It was the most magical sight I ever saw or experienced in my life."

Fausta cocked her head. "Sister dear—if you could see your eyes—you are a woman in love. No wonder you're having a meltdown. Are you going to tell Arnaud?"

Donetta wheeled around. "I'm not sure what I'm going to do, because there's so much more you don't know."

"That doesn't sound good."

"To be honest, I'm in a complete daze." She started pacing the parquet floor and then stopped. "I'm going to tell you something that can't go beyond this room."

"As if it would."

"I'm sorry, Fausta. It's just that so many lives could be upset by what went on between me and Enrico that I'm frightened."

"If you don't hurry and tell me, I don't think my heart will be able to take it."

Donetta drew in a deep breath. "On our way to the airport, I learned Enrico has plans to get married."

"What?"

She put up her hands. "Hear me out." In the next few minutes she explained what Enrico had told her in the limo. After she'd finished telling her everything, Fausta grasped her arms.

"Oh, my gosh. Enrico was talking about *you* the whole time! He wants to marry *you* and share his throne with *you*!" She shook her gently before letting her go. "Donetta, your lifelong dream to be queen could come true if you marry him!

"Look at what happened the second he saw you in Madrid. You get an invitation to a *concorso* from him in his own country. You've just been with him and love is written all over you. The two of you were crazy about each other back in your teens. I remember the day the letters stopped coming. It broke your heart."

"That's true, Fausta. It killed me that he stopped writing to me. But that's all over now. He doesn't love me. Enrico made it clear it would be a marriage in name only."

A frown marred her brow. "I don't believe it."

"I'm afraid he's changed."

"Look at me and tell me he didn't kiss you while you were camping."

Donetta turned aside. "We did, and I encouraged it. I know he's attracted to me, but that doesn't mean he's madly in love." She shook her head. "I guess… I don't trust that he loves me. Otherwise he would have asked me to marry him after he came back from the university."

"But if it isn't love, what other reason

could there be for him to reveal you're the one he wants to marry?"

"He spelled it out. His country has problems dealing with corruption. He wants a queen who will be professional and rule while he does his own work away from the palace."

"What about children?"

"Maybe he doesn't want them."

"But *you* do."

"I know. I'm so confused and shocked that he proposed."

"What are you going to do? I can see you're gutted."

"Even if I told Enrico I would marry him, neither his mother nor our parents would allow it to happen."

"But the point is, I can tell that you *want* to accept his proposal."

Donetta turned a tear-stained face to her sister. "You probably think I'm crazy to consider marrying Enrico when he's not in love with me. But Arnaud isn't in love with me, either, and—"

"And you'd rather marry the man *you* love," Fausta interrupted.

She nodded her head. "Yes. Arnaud needs to be free of me and have time to meet someone he can truly love. But if Enrico and I tell our parents, it could make Papà's illness worse and cause a terrible rift between Enrico and his mother that he has already warned me about."

"Yet he still wants you for his wife because he knows you will make a wonderful ruler. It's what you always dreamed of."

Donetta averted her eyes. "I thought I did once, but I'd rather have his love and his children."

"You really are in love to say something like that to me."

"I am."

"When are you going to give Enrico his answer?"

"First I have to tell Arnaud I can't marry him. No matter what happens between Enrico and me—maybe nothing—Arnaud needs to know it's over between us. He shouldn't be kept in the dark a minute longer."

"Agreed. Call him tonight and end it. Don't make him wait until tomorrow night. He'll appreciate your honesty. It's the only way to do this."

"You're right. What would I do if I couldn't talk to you, Fausta?" She hugged her. "I'm thinking of flying back to Vallefiore in the morning to talk to Enrico in person. My bag is still packed. Nothing this earthshaking can be discussed over the phone. I'll contact Giovanni. He can arrange for me and Enrico to talk in private without his mother knowing about it."

"Go for it, Donetta."

She smiled. "I wish you'd been there to see how Queen Teodora looked at me while we were watching the competition. Daggers flew at me. She's wanted Enrico to marry Valentina for years. I know in my heart she'll never give us her blessing, feud or not."

Fausta rolled her eyes. "It doesn't sound like Enrico is worried about that, and he isn't using his father's illness as an excuse to avoid marriage. He's asked you to marry him. He'll be king. Except for the feud between our countries, our parents can't be too unhappy about this. You'll be a real queen, something you've wanted all your life.

"It's almost like he has read your mind, but I know that's not possible unless you told him during one of the times you were together."

Donetta shook her head. "I would *never*

have told another soul but you and Lanza about that dream of mine. Did you tell Mia?"

"Even if I did, she would never breathe a word to anyone. In my opinion a miracle has happened to you. I'll drive you to the airport early in the morning before the parents are awake and cover for you until you contact them."

If this was out of the frying pan into the fire, then so be it. "You're a wonder!"

She hugged Fausta again before her sister left the apartment. Before she did anything else, Donetta alerted her pilot. Then phoned the Montedoro Lake Front Hotel on Lake Saracene to reserve a room for her for tomorrow. She requested that a car be sent to meet her jet. Once that was done, she sat down on the side of the bed to phone Arnaud.

"*Ma belle*—I didn't expect to hear from you tonight."

"Arnaud, I'm sorry to disturb you this late, but this call couldn't wait."

After a silence he said, "You sound so serious I know I'm not going to like it."

She swallowed hard. "It's very serious because we're talking marriage and neither of us is in love the way we should be. I can't marry you, Arnaud. It wouldn't be right for either of us and you know it!"

"You're still in love with someone else."

This was the time for honesty. "Yes. One day you'll fall hard for a woman who will feel the same way about you. I think you're a wonderful man. In my own way I do love you and wish you every happiness in the future."

"I can't say you didn't warn me."

"Take care, Arnaud."

"Be happy, Donetta."

After hanging up, she pressed the phone to her chest. Instead of feeling horrible, she felt relieved that both she and Arnaud had their freedom. It had been the right thing to do.

She packed another bag with some of her favorite clothes. Whatever happened after she reached Vallefiore, she wanted to be prepared.

After climbing into bed, she set her watch alarm for 5:30 a.m. but spent a restless night. The next morning she slipped out of the palace with Fausta, who drove her to the airport.

Donetta had no idea what kind of a reception she would get as she made the phone call to Giovanni en route. The blood pounded in her ears while she waited to reach him.

But she was met with fierce disappointment when she heard his voice mail.

Donetta left Enrico's cousin a message that she was on her way to Vallefiore and would be registered at the Montedoro Lake Front Hotel before long. If he could call her back at the number on this phone, she'd be grateful.

The steward served her a meal. For the rest of the flight Donetta sat there full of anxiety and excitement over what she was about to do. If they did decide to get married, she would have to remember that this was purely a business arrangement and she mustn't engage her feelings or show Enrico how she really felt.

CHAPTER FIVE

ENRICO SAT OUTSIDE the interrogation room at the police station in the village of Avezzano, Vallefiore. The angry man being questioned didn't know he was observed.

Through Enrico's undercover work and supervision, this was the latest of ten people from western Vallefiore being investigated for suspected involvement in corrupt practices. He'd already witnessed the interrogations of the mayor, his councillor and his assistant.

The four were facing charges including extortion, fraud and money laundering after Enrico had gathered evidence over the last two months. This particular investigation was linked to subcontracts awarded to build energy farms near the village. It was long past time to crack down on corruption in a major way.

At this point a total of ten people, including those from the next village of Caserta, were under investigation. Two of them were managers from a firm that had won the main contract to build one of the wind farms, installing sixty-three turbines.

The contract was worth 120 million euros, and the proceeds from them, he knew, were being channeled to offshore bank accounts. Enrico had indisputable proof they'd been illegally trying to get into the renewable energy sector for many years. Finally he'd heard enough to give the order for their arrests.

It was the only pleasure he'd known since Donetta had flown back to Domodossola yesterday. The fact that she'd gotten on the jet instead of running back to him and telling him what he needed to hear had dealt him a crushing blow.

He'd hoped his proposal would make her see she could rule with real power, but it wasn't meant to be. She was ambitious, incredibly capable, and he'd learned she had a hunger to be queen. Deep down he knew a marriage to Arnaud couldn't possibly fulfill her.

Trying to deal with his pain, he'd chosen

these couple of days to drive to Avezzano and get this investigation over. If he'd stayed at the palace, the walls would have closed in on him.

Now that he'd finished his work here, he was heading for Caserta, twelve miles away. He would find an isolated area to sleep out later tonight. He alerted his bodyguards he was leaving and went out to his Land Rover.

His sister Lia phoned to give him an update on their father. Ending the call, Enrico realized that his mother had pointedly refrained from speaking to him over the last couple of days. Clearly she was still upset about his relationship with Princess Donetta. But she didn't need to worry any longer. Donetta was gone from his life.

After a few miles the phone rang again. Hopefully, his cousin wasn't calling about an emergency that took him back to Saracene.

"Chè di nuovo?"

"Where are you?" Giovanni blurted without preamble.

"I'm driving to Caserta."

"Stop the car!"

Enrico frowned but pulled to the side of

the road. "What's going on?" After talking to Lia, he knew all was well back at the palace.

"You've got to turn around and come home immediately."

"Why?" He was in no mood to put out another fire.

"Because Donetta just flew in on the royal jet from Domodossola. She's registered at the Lake Front Hotel in the palm suite and—"

"Wait—" Enrico's heart had almost exploded out of his chest. "Say that again!"

"Donetta is here in Saracene!"

He gasped. "How *could* she be?"

"I don't know. She left a message on my phone, but I haven't called her back yet. What do you want me to do?"

Enrico had to think. "I'd rather talk to her myself." *Santo cielo.* He was still trying to catch his breath. "I've turned around and am on my way home. I'll be there in forty minutes. Put a guard on her. Warn him he's not to let her out of his sight if she leaves her room! Don't tell him who she is."

"You think I'm crazy? Your mother would explode. I'll take care of it right now."

"I owe you, cousin."

Driving over the speed limit, Enrico made

one vital phone call before reaching the hotel in record time. It was midafternoon when he raced inside to her suite on the second floor. One of the palace guards stood outside the door.

"Your Highness."

"Thanks for your help." His heart refused to calm down. "You can go now."

After the guard nodded and disappeared, Enrico knocked.

"Chi è?"

That was her voice. She *really* was here. "Why don't you open the door and find out?"

"Enrico—" He heard the incredulity in her voice.

When the door opened, the exquisite sight of Donetta dressed in casual pants and a silky plum-colored blouse robbed Enrico of coherent thought. Disbelieving, he leaned against the doorjamb for support. All he wanted to do was crush her in his arms, but he didn't dare do that.

"Donetta, I don't understand. Why did you come back?"

Her eyes blazed a seafoam green. "Did I wait too long to tell you I'll marry you?"

How he loved this woman! "You've just

made me the happiest man on the planet."
He struggled to catch his breath.

"I phoned Arnaud last night and told him
I couldn't be his wife."

Grazie a Dio. His dream was coming true.

Enrico closed the door behind him and
walked into the sitting room. "When you
climbed those steps yesterday, I thought
I'd seen the last of you. I never want to live
through agony like that again. Do your parents know where you are?"

"My sister drove me to the airport early
this morning. By now they're probably aware
I've flown here. I've burned my bridges and
am on my own."

What more could he have asked for? She'd
wanted to rule with him more than marry
Arnaud. Giovanni's informant had gotten
that part of the gossip right.

"Your mother has no idea you've asked me
to marry you, does she, Enrico?"

"No, but her spies keep her informed and
by now she has no doubt heard you've come
back to Vallefiore."

"I'm sure of it," Donetta murmured.

"Which means we need to get married
ASAP. To hell with the feud between our two

countries. I plan to bring it to an end once I'm king. We have to make arrangements fast so it'll be a fait accompli before anyone tries to stop us. The palace priest is a close friend of mine and will perform the ceremony in the palace chapel tomorrow. He'll provide the two needed witnesses."

"I hope you're sure about this, Enrico, because there's no going back."

"Why do you think I invited you to the *concorso* in the first place? My plan has been to marry you for a long time. I'll admit it threw me when you said you were planning to marry Arnaud, but it didn't change my hope to make you my queen. I couldn't let you fly back to Domodossola until you knew I wanted you to share the throne with me."

She rubbed her hands absently against her womanly hips. "When I was younger, I wanted to change the rules of succession in Domodossola and become queen. That dream could never have happened. But after you asked me to rule equally with you, I thought about it all the way home and decided I wanted to say yes to you."

"Suddenly my life is worth living again."

Enrico was overjoyed his plan had worked. There were so many things he wanted to tell her, but he needed to make immediate plans for their marriage first.

"Though we can't rewrite the past, there's nothing to prevent us from building an exciting future. Before it gets any later, and the shops close, I'm going to phone my sister Lia and ask her to buy you a wedding dress. No one will question what she's doing and she'll bring it here."

"She won't mind? Does she know anything about me?"

"Only that she saw you at the *concorso* and was introduced to you. But she's going to find out now, and she can be trusted. While I do that, why don't you order some dinner for us from the restaurant. Anything you think we'll want."

"All right."

While she reached for the room phone, he pulled out his cell to make the call. "Lia?"

"*Ehi!* Are you still worried about Papà?"

"No, I'm calling for an entirely different reason and you can't breathe a word to a soul except Marcello."

"This sounds serious."

"It is. The woman I'm going to marry has come back to Vallefiore."

"What?"

"You heard me."

"It's Princess Donetta, isn't it?"

"Yes."

"I *knew* it when I saw the two of you at the *concorso*. Neither of you were aware anyone else existed."

"You're right about that." She was the love of his life.

"Are you really getting married?" she cried for joy.

"Yes."

"I knew you'd never marry Valentina."

"I couldn't."

"It's going to hurt Mamma, but this isn't the Middle Ages and you deserve to marry the woman you love."

His eyes closed tightly for a moment. "Amen. Right now I need your help."

"You've got it."

"Donetta needs a wedding dress. We'll be getting married in the palace chapel tomorrow. Find her the right outfit in keeping with a ceremony taking place in secret. If you hurry, you can get to the shops before they close. She's staying at the Lake Front Hotel in the palm suite on the second floor. I'll be waiting for you."

"This is going to be so much fun, *fratello caro*. The princess is gorgeous."

His sister didn't know the half of it. "I can always count on you, Lia. But remember, not a word to Mamma."

"And start a war when we know a marriage between Donetta's country and ours is forbidden?" she cried. "Eventually Mamma will find out and have to live with it, but it will be *after* the fact and I couldn't be happier."

"Love you, Lia. *Grazie*."

"Ciao."

He hung up and turned to Donetta, who looked so divine he couldn't believe she was going to be his wife. "Lia will be here in a couple of hours."

"That's so kind of her. She must be shocked."

"She's thrilled I'm getting married to the woman I want to rule with me. You should have heard the joy in her voice."

"Fausta is excited for me, too."

Enrico wanted to envelop her in his arms, but he would show her how he really felt after they got married and went away. There was a knock on the door. "That'll be room service."

"I'll get it," Donetta volunteered. "I'm sure the staff knows you and your security are here, but you should still keep out of sight."

"You're right." He disappeared in the bedroom and shut the door.

Another minute and she said, "You can come out now, Enrico."

A tray of food had been set on the small round table in the sitting room. He sat on the chair opposite her. "I can't believe we're together at last, for good. Our past is behind us."

Suddenly he was starving and ate two of the hotel's signature club sandwiches before swallowing his coffee. "After the ceremony, we'll come back here while you change. Once we talk to your parents, we'll have brunch with my parents."

"It's going to be hard facing them."

"Maybe not as bad as you think. Except for the feud, they have no reason to dislike either of us once we all get acquainted."

Donetta laughed gently. "I agree, but our secret marriage will come as a blow."

"While they try to recover, we'll be on our honeymoon."

"Honeymoon?"

"Of course. We need one, don't you think?" He had plans for them.

"Where will we go?"

"Do you mind if I surprise you?"

"Of course not. I'm just thankful that Fausta is with my parents and they know exactly what has happened. But it won't take away their pain from not being at our ceremony."

"But this is what we have to do in order to be married. In the end both families will come around."

"I admire your optimism." She put down her coffee cup. "What about your mother, Enrico? When she hears our news, she'll need your father's support."

He reached for her hand and kissed the palm. "You know very well she'll take it badly. We know what her dream has been. But she'll have my sisters to comfort her and help her to understand."

She lifted anxious green eyes to him. "How are we going to deal with all this?"

"By becoming man and wife." As he said

it, they both heard a knock on the door. "That'll be Lia."

"Do you need me to go in the bedroom?"

"No." He got up from the table. "If I know my sister, she can't wait to welcome you to the family." Enrico hurried to answer the door.

Lia was loaded with packages. "It looks like you bought out the store." He kissed her cheek. "Bless you for coming to our rescue." Enrico brought everything into the sitting room and put her purchases on the couch.

Donetta came closer. "Princess Lia? How do I thank you for what you've done?"

Enrico's brown-eyed sister smiled and stepped forward to kiss Donetta's cheek. "It was my privilege. I'm so excited this day has come I can hardly believe it."

Donetta kissed her back. "I'm still reeling. Your brother and I have known each other since we were ten years old."

Lia let out a cry of surprise. "That long?"

She nodded. "We met at a *concorso* in England seventeen years ago."

Enrico smiled. "It was instant attraction."

"But you never said a word, *fratello*. No wonder you couldn't wait to go to every single one of them!" She laughed and turned to Donetta. "Maybe one day you'll tell me why you've kept it a secret, but I won't stay here any longer to find out. You two need time alone."

Donetta's eyes misted over. "Thank you from the bottom of my heart."

Lia blew a kiss to both of them and disappeared. The second she'd left the suite Donetta cried, "She's wonderful!"

"She and Catarina will always be on our side."

"I have news for you, Enrico. I know my sisters will love you. In fact I need to phone Fausta before another minute goes by, to thank her and find out how my parents are coping."

"You do that while I call Giovanni."

She hurried into the bedroom and sat down on the side of the bed to call Fausta.

"Donetta—thank goodness you've called at last!"

"I'm so relieved to talk to you. If the parents know everything already, I'm afraid to ask if I gave Papà a heart attack."

"I think Mamma took it harder than he did."

"Was it horrible, Fausta?"

"The second I came back from the airport Mamma called me to come to their sitting room. They knew something serious was going on. After I explained that you'd always been in love with Enrico and he'd wanted to marry you but thought it was hopeless, she sobbed and Papà's eyes watered.

"He thought for a minute and then said, 'I'll be damned. I didn't think there was a man alive who could win my daughter's love to the point she would do anything to be with him.'"

"He said that?" Donetta cried in shock and surprise.

"Cross my heart. If you want my opinion, I don't think he was that upset when I told him everything. He knows you weren't in love with Arnaud."

Donetta wiped the moisture off her face. She realized her father had pressed her to marry Arnaud because he didn't want her to go through life alone. Deep down she knew that and loved him for it. "Oh, Fausta—"

"Whatever they talked about after that was in private. But when I told Mamma about your history with Enrico, she was amazed when I told her that I saw for myself that the two of you were in love."

"I'm sure that came as a shock."

"Papà seems in surprisingly good spirits. Especially when I told him what you said about Enrico planning to have the problem of the old feud investigated and put to rest. He and Mamma have been in their apartment ever since. Honestly, I think everything is going to be all right."

"Only because you were there to intervene for me. I love you so much, Fausta."

"I love you, too, and I was talking to Lanza earlier about everything. She said that after what she and Stefano went through when Alberto died before they found happiness together, they both agree it won't be long before Arnaud is going to be thankful for what you did.

"He's been spared a life of unhappiness. Stefano will tell you himself that what you did today was a courageous act he admired, even if it caused pain at the time."

Her phone was dripping wet. "Thank you for telling me that."

"Both Lanza and I are overjoyed you're going to marry Enrico."

"Your support means everything to me. I know you're both going to be crazy about him when you get acquainted with him. Fausta? If there's an opportunity, will you let the parents know we'll be phoning them in the morning, unless you think tonight would be better."

"I think tomorrow will be fine," Fausta answered. "It'll give Mamma time to warm to the idea that when Enrico is crowned king of Vallefiore, you'll be the queen. Know what I mean?"

Donetta knew exactly what she meant. She'd become a real queen in her own right once she married Enrico. But all she wanted was her husband's love.

A knock on the door brought her to her feet. "I'll talk to you soon. *Buona notte.*"

She dashed to the door and threw it open. Enrico's black eyes searched hers. "How did it go?"

"Much better than I could have hoped for."

"*Grazie a Dio.* I want to stay with you all night, but Mamma has her own news sources. Giovanni told me word has reached her that the royal jet from Domodossola flew in and you are staying here at the hotel. I wouldn't be surprised if she had already put her own construction on everything."

She sucked in her breath. "Anything is possible."

"For that reason I'm going to go back to the palace for the night, but I'll be here first thing in the morning. We'll grab a quick breakfast and head for the chapel. When it's over, we'll come back here to change clothes and talk to your parents. Afterward we'll brunch with my parents before we leave on our honeymoon."

Enrico reached for her and gave her a warm kiss on her lips, his first demonstration of affection, but it wasn't like that morning when they'd watched the wild horses.

"You know I don't want to leave when there's so much to talk about. That's why our wedding needs to happen tomorrow. I don't want to give my mother time to come up with a reason to delay our wedding. Knowing her feelings, she would try."

Donetta nodded and followed him to the door of her suite. "I'll see you in the morning. Come early," she begged.

"You don't need to tell me that." He kissed

her cheek before striding swiftly down the hall on those long, powerful legs.

She couldn't wait for morning to come. Realizing she was getting married in about eight hours, she took out the wedding dress to inspect it. The Italian-designed gown had a simplicity Donetta loved. She held it up to her in front of the floor-length mirror of her hotel bedroom.

The dreamy white A-line gown in chiffon and alençon lace featured cap sleeves under lacy short sleeves and a scalloped scoop neckline. Bands of lace appliques adorned the skirt that swept the floor. On her head she would wear a shoulder length alençon lace mantilla.

Lia had picked a dress without a long train. It was the perfect choice. Donetta hadn't wanted anything extravagant like Lanza's gown. She wasn't getting married in the cathedral with the whole country her audience. There'd be no press release, no fanfare, no family in attendance.

Once she'd hung the dress in the closet, she undid all the packages including the hose and white shoes. Lia had excellent taste. Donetta loved everything the princess had bought for her.

After getting ready for bed she climbed under the covers, recalling her father's words. *I'll be damned. I didn't think there was a man alive who could win my daughter's love to the point she would do anything to be with him.*

That was exactly what Donetta had done, because Enrico was her heart's desire, even if he didn't love her back in the same way.

Tears trickled out of the corners of her eyes.

You can't have everything you want, Donetta. But half a loaf is better than marrying the wrong man.

When Enrico knocked on Donetta's door at eight in the morning, he was stunned by the sight of her in the white wedding dress that fit her so well it could have been made for her. He kissed her cheek. She smelled like roses. Beneath her lace mantilla, those light green eyes seemed illuminated. Frosted pink lipstick glistened on her beautiful mouth.

"Whether you know it or not, you're the most gorgeous princess on the planet."

"Thank you," she answered, sounding slightly breathless.

"Are you ready to become my bride?"

The smile he remembered from years ago answered his question. "What do *you* think? You're very handsome in that white dress suit and blue sash. The personification of a perfect prince."

"*Grazie*, but no one cares about the groom. This is your day. I intend to be the best husband I can be to you."

"I'll do everything in my power to be the queen you're hoping for."

"You'll be exceptional. Shall we leave for the chapel?"

"Yes, unless you're hungry and need to eat first. There are rolls and fruit on the table."

"I can't eat. I'm too excited to marry you. The limo is waiting out in the back to take us to the chapel."

She reached for the white satin clutch bag that Lia had thoughtfully bought to go with the gown and left the room with him. They descended the staircase and walked down a hall past some shocked guests to the rear entrance, where he helped her into the limo.

During the drive to the chapel they sat across from each other. The smoky glass prevented onlookers from seeing them seated on the inside.

He smiled at her. "Everyone recognizes the hood ornament's royal crest. By the time we drive back to the hotel, our wedding will no longer be a secret."

She nodded. "I'm tired of secrets."

"We were partners in crime and got away with it for years. Once we're married, we'll never have to worry about it again."

"Except that we're committing the worst crime of all by merging a modern-day Montague with a Capulet."

"It won't be a crime once I'm king, *bellissima*. I've already laid the groundwork to investigate what really happened two hundred years ago. When I have evidence, I'll show it to your father. It'll be my gift to him for allowing me to marry his daughter."

Donetta's eyes misted over. "I'm only sorry your father doesn't realize his son is being married this morning."

"Maybe when we have brunch with him and announce our news, he'll know somehow. One look at you and he'll wonder why it took me so long."

"I'm still worried about your mother's reaction, Enrico."

"She'll recover. We just have to give her

time. Right now I'm ready to take the biggest step of my life with the woman who caught my eye all those years ago."

The limo slowed to a stop. "We've arrived outside the private entrance to the chapel. Once we walk inside, there's no going back. Any second thoughts?"

She stared into his eyes. "None."

CHAPTER SIX

DONETTA WAS STUNNED by the the palace chapel, a a beautiful creation of Moorish design. The interior glowed with lighted candles as they walked arm in arm on ancient tiled floors of fantastic colors and intricate motifs toward the priest in his black robes. In these surroundings that hinted at both the Moorish and Ottoman Empires, she felt transported to the Ottoman Empire.

Holding on to Enrico's arm, she passed under one ornately designed arch after another. Each one was covered with lacelike patterns leading to stained glass windows of mosaic artisanship set in flower shapes.

Chairs with velvet cushions were placed on either side of the aisle. The two witnesses sat on the front seats.

Like everything he did, Enrico had side-stepped the rules. He explained he'd asked the elderly priest to keep the ceremony short for secrecy until they could announce their news to both sets of parents.

The priest didn't give a long sermon about marriage. What he told them was to be honest with each other, trust and love each other. Those were vows Donetta could keep with all her heart.

She was excited beyond belief when the priest came to the last part. Enrico slid the Montedoro-crested gold wedding band on her finger. To her chagrin she had no ring for him, but that was her next priority.

"I now pronounce you, Enrico da Francesca di Montedoro, and you, Louisa Regina Donetta Rossiano, husband and wife, in the name of the Father, the Son and the Holy Spirit. Amen. You may kiss your bride, Enrico."

It was the most natural thing in the world to melt into his arms after taking her vows and lift her mouth to his the way she'd done in the mountains. Donetta had to restrain her passion from here on out since he'd said their marriage would be in name only. But he'd said he loved her and she knew he'd chosen her for his bride. Now she was married to the man she loved. No more separations. Together *forever*.

They thanked the priest and signed the marriage document before walking back out to the waiting limo. This time when they sat opposite each other, he grasped her hands. "We've done it, Signora Montedoro. It's what I've wanted for so long."

"I confess that I hoped to become your wife while you were away at university, but never thought I'd see this day, Signor Montedoro."

From his pocket he pulled out a three-carat blue-white diamond set in white gold and put the ring on her finger next to the wedding band. She gasped. "I bought this diamond after college, planning to give it to you. I didn't want to present you with one of the family jewels. You need to have your own."

"Enrico."

"After I saw you in Madrid, I had it set in white gold to match your hair."

She held up her hand. "I adore it!"

The limo pulled up to the rear entrance of the hotel. "It's vital Mamma sees evidence of our ceremony and knows how important you are to me. Hopefully, when my father looks at these rings, something will register in his brain."

"I could pray for that. He has to be an outstanding father to have raised a son like you."

"You're very sweet, Donetta. We were always in lockstep. He would welcome you with open arms if it were possible. Let's hurry inside so you can change, and then we'll make that phone call to your parents."

Within a few minutes they reached her hotel room and she changed out of her wedding finery into a silky white blouse and print skirt of white and café-au-lait. When she came out of the bedroom, she found him eating.

They walked over to the couch and sat down while she reached for her phone.

"It's going to be all right." Enrico could probably tell she was trembling.

She nodded and pushed the speed dial. "It's ringing. I've put it on speaker."

"Donetta, darling?" came her mother's voice after the first ring. "The girls told us you would be calling this morning. Your father is right here."

Donetta clutched his hand. "Enrico is with me, too. We're on speaker."

"So are we."

"I don't know where to start except to tell you both I love you and always will. What I did yesterday has hurt everyone and I don't expect forgiveness. But when I came to Vallefiore and spent time with Enrico, I knew I couldn't marry Arnaud because it was Enrico I loved."

"As I love Donetta," Enrico broke in. "We've been in love for years, but my father has been plagued with Alzheimer's since I was at university." His voice rang with the truth, thrilling her. "I had to fully support him and couldn't go after Donetta until very recently. Once we saw each other again, we knew how we felt, but she was already promised to Prince Arnaud.

"I know Prince Arnaud must be disappointed. I hope that he recovers soon. We're calling you this morning to let you know that Donetta and I were just married in the palace chapel by our family priest. Later today we'll be meeting with my mother to get her blessing. I hope we have yours."

"You have it," Donetta's father interjected in a choked voice. "Only a woman madly in love would do what you did, Donetta. We want your happiness."

By now she was in tears. "Thank you."

"Donetta?" her mother chimed in. "We love you, and welcome you to the family, Enrico."

Enrico swallowed hard. "That means more to me than you will ever know. Before long the coronation will take place and we'll want your whole family here with us."

"We'll be waiting with excitement for that day. Thank you for giving us this marvelous news."

"I love you and Papà," Donetta said before they both heard the click. She buried her face in her hands.

Enrico put his arm around her shoulders. "Your parents are remarkable, *bellissima*."

"They are." She lifted her head. "So are you. The things you said to them reassured them as nothing else could."

Enrico kissed the side of her wet face. "Let's go to the palace. We'll have brunch in the small dining room with my parents. My father will have been wheeled in, but he never talks, so Mamma will preside. I love her and can only hope she'll be as gracious as your parents. Shall we go?"

Donetta reached for her handbag and he walked her out to the waiting limo with its tinted glass. After telling the driver to take them to the palace, he slid in next to her and put his arm around her again.

"After you left, I was in the depths of despair. I drove out of the city not knowing whether to work or go crazy. I couldn't have dreamed my cousin would phone and tell me your jet had arrived in Saracene. For a moment I thought I was hallucinating, but you're here and real."

"I can hardly believe it myself. It was like a dream yesterday when I heard you say you wanted to marry me. So much has happened since then that I'm still trying to take it all in."

"After we meet with my parents, we'll have all the time we want and need to get used to the idea that we belong to each other at last."

CHAPTER SEVEN

DONETTA REALLY DID belong to him now! The boy she'd been attracted to years ago had grown up to become the man she'd just married. But this was no fairy tale. They were on their way to tell his parents. Enrico's mother wouldn't react the way Donetta's parents had done. She needed to be prepared for fireworks.

The trip to the palace didn't take long. He helped her out of the limo and escorted her up the steps to the area reserved for the business of the king. The official flag of the country hung outside the throne room. Soon, this was where she would start to govern the affairs of the country with him. The feeling was surreal.

Further down the hall he led her up a staircase to the second floor, where they came to the small dining room. According to Enrico,

the man who stood outside the opened double doors was his father's caregiver. Enrico
patted his arm as they entered.

The king, impeccably dressed and
groomed in a gray suit and white shirt, sat
in a wheelchair at the head of the oval table,
with his head slightly drooped. His black hair
was peppered with a lot of gray.

Enrico drew Donetta with him and leaned
over. "Papà? This is my wife, Princess Donetta Rossiano of Domodossola." He turned
to her. "Donetta? Please meet my father,
King Nuncio."

Donetta was so moved to witness the love
Enrico showed his father that she had to clear
her throat to speak. "It's one of the greatest
honors of my life to meet you, Your Majesty.
I've heard great things about you and know
they're all true because I see those same wonderful qualities in your son, whom I love."

She'd never said those words to Enrico,
but they'd slipped out now.

Of course there was no response from his
father, but like Enrico, she hoped that something about this moment had reached a part
of him that knew what was going on.

When she lifted her head, she saw the

queen in the doorway, wearing a rose-colored two-piece suit. Again Donetta was reminded that Enrico had inherited attractive traits from both parents. "Your Majesty." She curtsied to her.

"Princess Rossiano." Just like that day at the *concorso*, Donetta saw no smile in the queen's eyes. This woman was her new mother-in-law.

Enrico accompanied his mother to the table, where he seated her on her husband's left side. Then he cupped Donetta's elbow, took her around and helped her into a chair before he took his place between her and the king.

Two kitchen staff waited on them, pouring coffee and serving an elaborate brunch that included a variety of mouthwatering cut melons. Donetta made the effort to eat, but her nerves had taken away her appetite.

"Papà? Mamma? I asked the two of you to join with Donetta and me to celebrate our marriage."

An audible gasp came out of his mother. Her face lost color, but Enrico kept going. "I've loved Donetta for years and now she has done me the honor of marrying me."

He'd said the same thing to her parents, convincing her he loved her as fiercely as she loved him.

His mother's brown eyes pierced Donetta. "You were promised to Prince Arnaud." Her voice sounded totally shaken.

Knowing this moment had to come, Donetta girded up her courage. Enrico gripped her hand to give her his support. "I realized at the last moment that I couldn't marry Arnaud when I knew I loved Enrico."

"Have you always been this dishonorable to your parents?"

Enrico squeezed her hand harder to give her courage. "To have married Arnaud would have been wrong, Your Majesty. But I know I've put everyone through agony and will suffer for it for a long time. All I can hope is that the day will come when you'll be able to be happy about what has happened and accept me."

"Mamma—" Enrico broke in. "I spoke to the priest yesterday. Because of Papà's illness, he understood the urgency and agreed to marry us this morning. We had a private ceremony in the palace chapel with only two witnesses chosen by the priest."

The queen's eyes narrowed. "In other words, he dispensed with protocol and waived the banns so you could have your heart's desire."

Donetta trembled.

"We've waited too long as it is, Mamma."

"Of course you knew you would never have our permission, Enrico. Have you no decency toward Valentina and her family? They'll be shattered when they hear this news."

"Valentina knows I've never loved her. If anything she'll be relieved and now have a chance to meet a man who will love her as she deserves."

"She loves *you!*"

"Love has to be reciprocated. You know that. I could never have married her when I've been in love with Donetta for years. We should have been man and wife long ago, but circumstances prevented it before now."

"How easily you say that when you realize this marriage of yours is forbidden!"

"Only if you decide it is. Something that happened two hundred years ago should have been fixed long before now. I've already started to rectify the situation as we speak."

"Well, *I* intend to do something about it now. Since you didn't choose Princess Valentina for your bride, I won't allow the cabinet to let you be crowned king. *There'll be no coronation!*"

Donetta shuddered. The queen's words couldn't have been more cruel, but Enrico didn't act fazed. His father made no sound or motion.

"Thank you for meeting us for brunch, Mamma. I'll have to thank the chef for outdoing herself. Now Donetta and I ask to be excused so we can leave on our honeymoon. If you need anything while we're gone, Lia and Catarina will be on hand. In case of an emergency, Giovanni will let us know in an instant."

Another strange sound escaped his mother's lips. A part of Donetta felt horribly sorry for his mother. The queen was in so much pain and needed the king, who was helpless at this point.

"Before we go, may I help you push Father into the sunroom first?"

"No thank you," came his mother's comment. "I'll do it myself when I've finished my coffee."

Donetta could see where Enrico had inherited his spine. Both of them were major forces. The whole situation was a nightmare.

Enrico helped Donetta from the table. When they reached the doorway, he left her side long enough to go back and kiss both parents on the cheek. After returning, he grabbed Donetta's hand and they left the dining room.

He walked her to the main floor of the palace and down a hall to one of the entrances. "We'll take my Land Rover."

After they got in, she put a hand on his arm before he could start the engine.

"Enrico—we have to talk."

"I knew my mother would hurt you. I'm so sorry."

She shook her head. "You're the one I'm worried about. But I understand she can't help but be disappointed over what has happened."

"Except that she knew I never loved Valentina or planned to marry her. When she realizes how happy we are, she'll come around."

"But the protocol in your country dictates the banns be read four months prior to the marriage."

He grinned. "How do you know that?"

"Because I looked it up after the *concorso* in France."

"We both had marriage on our minds even then."

She nodded. "You told me how strict she is."

"You handled her beautifully. But this is *our* marriage, not hers." He started the car that had been packed with her bags and they left the palatial estate. "Have I thanked you for being so wonderful to my father?"

"The poor dear man. There needs to be a cure for Alzheimer's," she said in a tremulous voice. "I feel so sorry for your mother, too. I've heard that the spouse feels like he or she has already lost their life's partner. She must have been grieving for a long time."

"I know she has." His voice grated.

"Your father is very handsome. Now I know where you get your looks. When we were at the *concorso*, I noticed that you and your sisters resemble your lovely mother, too. One day I hope she'll be able to forget the pain."

"I guarantee it. But right now we need to

talk about a honeymoon. We'll do anything you want."

Her heart raced. "You mean you haven't already planned it?"

"Even if I have, I'm prepared to make alterations. I'll do anything for you. Tell me what you'd love to do most."

"Could we go camping and hiking in the mountains and at a lake so I can catch fish?"

He let out a whoop of delight.

"I take it you've already set everything up."

"I knew there was a reason why I wanted to marry you."

She couldn't take her eyes off him. "The first time I saw you ride your horse, I was only ten, but I knew I wanted to get to know you. Young Prince Enrico had a presence even then. No other boy ever interested me after that."

"Not even Arnaud?"

"You know he didn't. My parents pressured me the way your mother has pressured you about Valentina. When I believed I'd never see you again, I decided to say yes to him in order to have children one day. Children bring happiness."

He reached for her hand. "We're going to have more happiness than you can imagine, *bellissima*."

Enrico's favorite waterfall came into view, eliciting a satisfying cry from his exquisite bride of six hours.

But this time he drove down a semi-hidden road that led to the pool below, where he'd planned a surprise for her that had been in his mind for years. She'd wanted to camp out and she was going to get her wish.

Yesterday he'd asked Giovanni to pitch a black-and-tan-striped Moorish tent on the sandbar. With two small windows for light and ventilation, it had been set up to offer Donetta the rich luxury she deserved. His cousin had gathered helpers who'd turned the interior into a sumptuous bedroom with carpets and a bathroom with every amenity for two lovers.

Enrico had sent their luggage on ahead. A small table and chairs had been placed in one end. Giovanni had promised him coolers of food and a lighted oil lamp to greet them by the time they arrived that night.

During the day they could sunbathe all

they wanted. At night they would moon-bathe to their hearts' content, but he intended to make love to his wife in the privacy of their own boudoir for hour upon hour.

"Enrico—" she gasped when they reached their destination. "Oh, that tent—the pool and waterfall—it's absolutely enchanting with the moon shining down, like something out of *Arabian Nights*."

That was the idea. With his heart beating wildly, he got out of the Land Rover and walked around to her side. After opening her door, he swept her in his arms and carried her inside their tent, which would be their home away from home for as long as they wanted.

Another cry escaped her lips as she looked around the semi-dark interior in startled disbelief. Her eyes glowed that amazing green he loved so much. "You've created paradise for us."

"I love you, Donetta."

She stared at him strangely. "What are you saying?"

"I mean I really love you."

"But I thought—"

"Did you honestly think our marriage

would be in name only?" he fired. "The only reason I said it was because I was afraid if I told you how I really felt, you might feel I wasn't telling the truth after five years' absence.

"But that's history now. No more thinking, *amata*. I love you and want you. After our campout, I know you want me, too."

"I've never been able to hide anything from you. Oh, Enrico—you don't know how long I've been waiting for this, dying inside because I feared it would never happen. Love me, darling, and never stop."

She didn't need to worry about that. He carried her to the huge bed with its silk coverings and cushions, then followed her down. It was heaven to be able to plunge his hands into her silvery gold hair and kiss every inch of her.

Their mouths took over, exhibiting the fire and hunger that had been building since her arrival in Vallefiore for the *concorso*. No longer needing to hold back, they began the age-old ritual of bringing each other unimaginable pleasure.

Throughout the night and into the morning they experienced pure rapture, but now she was asleep with their legs tangled. Donetta was the most giving, loving woman a man could ask for. And she was *so* gorgeous in every way it hurt to look at her.

Even at ten years of age, he'd felt her pull on him. Every year after that she had grown more beautiful and haunted his dreams. There'd been too many years of separation. They would still be apart if she hadn't found the courage to fly back to him. He marveled that she'd been so strong.

It was that strength of character he'd admired so much after meeting her years ago. Now she was his wife and their long wait was finally over. The knowledge that she loved him filled him with a surfeit of emotion. He couldn't help pulling her closer, causing her eyes to open.

"Good morning, *mia sposa.*"

She smiled. "How long have you been awake?"

He traced the singing line of her mouth with his finger. "Long enough to want to make love to you all over again."

"I was just dreaming about you. I need you to kiss me or I won't be able to bear it."

On a groan of pleasure he fulfilled her

wishes as they tried to satisfy their insatiable desire for each other. Enrico hadn't thought it possible to live on love, but his wedding night with Donetta had transformed his vision of what it was like to be married to the right woman.

An hour later she eased out of his arms and reached for the robe she'd put at the side of the bed. "I'm going to look in the coolers and serve you breakfast in bed."

"I don't need food."

"Oh, yes, you do. Stay right there. I love that picture of you tangled in the sheets like my own drop-dead gorgeous Ali Pasha of Vallefiore. I'm your captive slave, eager to grant you your slightest desire. After watching you at brunch, I happen to know you love golden honeydew melon."

He watched her open the cooler and pull one out. After she cut it, she brought two big slices on a plate for them to eat. Enrico took a bite of one and couldn't stop. "It's almost as delicious as you are."

"I'll be right back." When she returned, she'd brought croissants filled with ham and cheese, plus two bottles of blood orange juice. They ate and drank their fill before he moved the plates to the floor. With a wicked smile he said, "Get back in bed with me."

"You mean you're not satisfied yet?" she teased.

"Are *you*, Your Highness?"

She removed her robe and slid in bed next to him. "I guess you'll have to find out."

Enrico caught her to him, so madly in love with her he didn't know how he'd existed this long without her. It wasn't until much later when he told her he wanted to go swimming with her. "I brought a bikini for you, but whether you wear it or not is your choice." He grinned.

"I think with the amount of security guarding us, I'll play it safe. As for you…" She rolled her eyes and slipped out of bed to get ready.

He couldn't take his eyes off her. "Both our suits are in the silver suitcase, *cara*."

She opened it and tossed him the black trunks before she disappeared behind the curtain that hid the makeshift bathroom. He took advantage of the time to put them on.

When she emerged in the black bikini he'd chosen for her, he let out a wolf whistle that drove her straight out of the tent, laughing.

He was right behind her and welcomed the hot sun before running into the pool of water to catch up with her. But she was fast and an excellent swimmer. Her athleticism made her exciting to be with.

They played at the base of the waterfall for an hour. When they were both worn out with water fights, he pulled her from the pool and they lay down on the sand to soak up the sun. In time it got hot enough he started to worry about her.

"I think we should go in or you're going to get a sunburn. We can't have that. Come on." He helped her to her feet and led her into the water so they could wash off the sand.

She looped her arms around his neck. "I didn't know I could be this happy."

"Tell me about it." Enrico was so enamored of her he picked her up and carried her back to the tent. They couldn't remove their suits fast enough before falling into bed in a conflagration of need.

Darkness had fallen before Enrico had mercy on her and brought her dinner in bed. Once they'd eaten their fill of meat pies prepared in the palace kitchen, they lay on their sides feeding each other grapes and almonds until they were gone.

She smiled into his eyes. "You've spoiled me so terribly I've become a lovesick wanton and I'm afraid you'll get tired of me."

He growled against her throat. "If you can think that, then you're in for the surprise of your life." She'd fast become his addiction. He started to make love to her with an almost primitive need that led to another delirious night of ecstasy for both of them.

CHAPTER EIGHT

WHEN LIGHT ENTERED the tent, Donetta awakened first and lay there studying her painfully handsome husband. Between Enrico's black hair and olive skin, he looked like a god. This morning he had a five o'clock shadow. She rubbed her cheek against his jaw, adoring the feel of it.

He was such a manly man. As she'd always thought, he was a dishy hunk. There weren't enough adjectives to describe what his looks did to her and the way he made her feel. That first miraculous kiss he'd given her when she was sixteen had been a precursor to what had happened to her during the night.

She let out a sigh of sheer exultation and stretched, unaware Enrico had opened his eyes and was watching her intently. His lips curved upward. "What was that little sound about, *tesora*?"

"You're beholding a contented wife in every sense of the word."

"Only contented?" he asked in his deep voice.

"If I told you the whole truth, it would make you blush."

"This is getting better and better." In the next breath he gave her a long, deep kiss. When he finally lifted his head, he said, "Before I do anything else, I'm going to shave."

"You don't have to. I've been lying here enjoying the look and feel of your beard."

"I adore you for saying that, but you'll like me better without it. When I've finished, shall we go fishing this morning?"

She blinked. "You mean there are fish in the pool?"

"I make sure our lakes and streams are filled. We'll catch ourselves some mouthwatering trout and cook them on the grill outside the tent. Anglers prefer them."

"You're kidding—trout? I can't wait!"

The laughter she loved poured out of him as he got out of bed and headed for the bathroom. She scurried over to her suitcase for a pair of white shorts and a sleeveless print blouse. By the time Enrico emerged clean-shaven and dressed in shorts, she was ready.

He found some fishing poles and a tackle box, and they headed outside into a world of brilliant, hot sunshine. "I'll get the grill heating up first. Then we'll walk halfway around the pool, where the fish congregate in a deep hole."

The next hour turned into a world of enchantment for Donetta. Trying to imitate his expertise as a superior fly fisherman, she managed to catch a couple of ten-inchers. Enrico, of course, brought in several that were a foot long each.

"Few people come to this pool to fish, so they've grown large."

"This is so much fun I can't stand it!"

Thrilled with their catch, she helped him clean them on the shore. He found a stick to carry them and they walked back around to the grill. The divine smell of trout cooking filled the air. Once the fish were ready, they had a feast inside the tent along with more melon, rolls and fresh coffee, brewed from a coffee maker that Giovanni had thoughtfully provided.

"Never in my life have I been so happy, or

enjoyed a meal more than this, Enrico." Her eyes filled with tears. "Thank you, darling, for this wonderful honeymoon."

"It's a long way from over, *cara*. We've only just begun. Maybe tomorrow, if I can stand to take you away from our bed for a few hours, we'll hike above the waterfall. You'll see sights you won't believe. I want you to learn to love my country."

She got up and slid her arms around his shoulders, leaning over to kiss the side of his face. "It's mine, too, now, and I already do."

He pulled her onto his lap and grew sober for a moment. "I'm sorry my mother treated you the way she did."

"Please don't worry about it. Don't you think I understand? If anything, I worry you were hurt when she told you she wouldn't allow the coronation to take place."

"I'm not hurt about that, Donetta. My father is still alive. As long as he draws breath, he's still the king. But that doesn't change my plan for you and me to rule equally. I don't need to be crowned to put my wishes into action. The truth is, I'm going to need your help even more than I had anticipated."

Donetta could tell he meant it. "You know I want to help you any way I can. What has changed?"

He hugged her to him. "I'll tell you everything, but not while we're on our honeymoon. This time for us is so precious. I don't want to spend one moment on anything but our love. Now that we've eaten, what would you like to do?"

"I'm afraid to tell you." She slid off his lap to clean up their breakfast dishes.

Enrico got up and slid his arms around her waist from behind. "Don't ever be afraid to tell me you want to go back to bed. I've been waiting for our breakfast to be over so I could ravage you."

She wheeled around. "Is that the truth?"

He put her over his shoulder in a fireman's lift and took her to bed. After he covered her body possessively, he kissed her neck. "Do you need any more proof?"

Over the next week Enrico showed her what it meant to be loved while he took her to his favorite parts of the island, and they hiked and slept out under the stars.

The next day they drove to the Ionian Sea to swim and dive. But as they left a grotto for a morning snack, Enrico's phone rang. The sound filled Donetta with dread.

She sat frozen on the sand while he answered it. By the lines that appeared around his compelling mouth, she knew he'd received bad news.

"That was Giovanni," he explained after hanging up. "He says my father fell and is in bed with a broken arm. The doctor has been there and he's doing fine, but my mother is beside herself."

"Of course she is."

He nodded gravely. "My parents need me, so I'm afraid we have to go back when it's the last thing I want to do."

Their honeymoon had been cut short, but she didn't dare complain. The pain of knowing they had to leave was excruciating. Donetta was an ungrateful wretch when she knew her husband had taken off more time than he should have.

They drove back to the waterfall to pack up and leave the tent that had become their love nest. But while she was looking for a pair of shorts, he pulled her down on the bed.

"You're not going anywhere yet," he said in a fierce tone.

* * *

After kissing her with abandon, Enrico made love to her one more time. But she knew they needed to leave. Donetta draped her arms around his neck. "You know the only reason I can bear to leave here is because I'm going home to live with you."

"Tell me about it."

They carried their belongings to the car. His black eyes impaled her. "Being able to have you in my life forever is all I ever wanted. Loving you as I do, to wake up every day in your arms from now on makes me feel reborn."

The Land Rover reached the road that led to Saracene. Donetta looked back at the waterfall one more time. One memory after another swamped her with emotions that made it hard to breathe. By the way Enrico grasped her hand and never let go, she knew he was experiencing them, too.

It was strange coming back to civilization. They'd been in a world of inexpressible pleasure. Entering the suburbs of the city seemed an intrusion on her whole psyche.

"It's hard for me, too." They were so in tune with each other's thoughts that Enrico had no trouble reading hers. "I promise we're going to get away often, *amore mio*."

The lake shimmered in the afternoon sun. Rising above it was the palace, with a commanding view of the water and the landscape. After they reached the estate, he drove them to his private entrance.

Enrico parked the Land Rover and walked around to open her door. He leaned in and gave her a long, sensuous kiss. "Welcome home, *squisita*."

Donetta felt his eagerness to take her to his apartment. *Their* apartment now. She was excited, too, never having seen it before.

He reached for their bags and escorted her inside the doors. A guard nodded to both of them. "Welcome home, Your Highness."

"*Grazie.*"

They walked up the staircase to the second floor, where another guard nodded. Donetta stayed close to Enrico as they walked down the hallway to a set of double doors. After he opened them, he put the bags down and turned to her. She knew what he was going to do before he picked her up and carried her over the threshold.

"You need to go to your parents."

"I will after I've shown you your new home."

Donetta had known his luxurious apartment would be fabulous. She loved it immediately, especially the view of the lake. He carried her around to every bedroom, the sitting room, study, dining room and kitchen.

"What do you think?"

"I know I'm going to be ecstatically happy here."

He let out a triumphant sound as his mouth closed over hers. They clung as if they'd never kissed before. When he eventually let her go he said, "I fear it's a man's domain, so I want you to decorate it any way you want."

"I love the light blue décor. The ambience is so *you*. The only thing I might change is to showcase all your riding trophies and pictures in a prominent place rather than a walk-in closet in one of the bedrooms. I remember your winning all of them."

"I'll agree to find a special spot as long as we ship your trophies here and display them together. They represent a big part of our lives."

She grasped his shoulders as she looked up at him. "Am I dreaming, or are we really standing in our own home?"

He lowered his mouth to kiss her again, but she finally pulled away from him. "You need to go."

"I promise I'll be back soon."

Donetta blew him a kiss, knowing he'd be gone a long time. By now the queen would know they'd returned.

She took the suitcases to Enrico's bedroom, which also had a spectacular view of the lake. Taking advantage of the time, she took a long shower and washed her hair. While she dried it, she phoned her family to let them know she was back and happier than she'd ever been in her life. Fausta had gone to town. Donetta would call her later.

She found jeans and a short-sleeved soft orange top to wear and then walked back to the living room. Donetta was drawn to the three framed oil paintings of his horses artistically arranged on part of one wall. Their names had been engraved on brass plaques below each one.

Donetta immediately recognized Malik and Rajah, the two horses that had garnered Enrico international championships. But she didn't know about the third one, which was a pony named Osman. All were black and came from the Sanfratellano breed.

"Osman means warrior in Arabic."

She turned around to see Enrico had come into the bedroom. "Darling—"

He put an arm around her waist. "My father gave me that pony when I was five years old. I felt like a warrior riding him around until my tenth birthday. At that point I'd outgrown him and was presented with Malik."

At the *concorso* in England, Enrico had told Donetta that the name Malik meant king in Arabic.

"The artist of these magnificent oils has captured their living, breathing essence. I wish I'd had paintings done of my horses."

"It's not too late. You have pictures. We could hire an artist."

"You're right, but it's not like painting them from real life. These are treasures."

"You're *my* real, live treasure."

She hugged him. "How's your father?"

"It's difficult to tell. He's been given pain medication and has to keep his arm in a sling."

"Poor thing. I bet your mother is happy you're back."

"She is, but she's insistent that I send a letter to Valentina and her parents right away. I told her I'd already planned to do it." He drew Donetta to the bedroom and sat down on the bed with her. "Now enough said about that."

"I agree. It would have been wrong for both of us to marry people we don't love, but all that is in the past."

"Tonight you and I have been asked to join Mamma and Papà for dinner at six thirty. But if—"

She put a finger to his lips. "Of course we'll go. I intend to do everything I can to win her trust."

"Donetta—" He crushed her to him.

For the rest of the afternoon the world receded to a place where only Enrico could take her. They would have been late for dinner if his cell phone hadn't rung.

Her husband groaned in protest. "I'd better answer it."

He reached for his shirt on the floor and found his phone. It was Giovanni. Clicking on, he said, *"Ciao, amico."* Enrico eyed her. "It's hard for us to come back, you know?"

Whatever his cousin said next produced

a frown, forcing him to leave the bed and head for his walk-in closet. After noticing the time, Donetta got up to take a quick shower.

By the time she'd dressed in a silky black-on-white printed short-sleeved dress and slipped into her white high heels, he'd reappeared in a navy robe.

His eyes played over her. "You look fabulous."

She eyed him anxiously. "Thank you, but I can tell something's wrong."

"Give me a minute to shower and change. Then we'll talk."

Enrico dressed in record time, putting on a casual light blue suit with an open-collared darker blue shirt. Ten minutes wouldn't give him much time for what he had to tell his wife, but he needed to prepare her after hearing Giovanni's latest news.

"Donetta?"

"I'm right here, enjoying the view." So she was. He joined her at the bedroom window. "There are a lot of sailboats out on the lake. Do you have one?"

He smiled. "I'm sure you know the answer to that. Have you done much sailing?"

"No. You'll have to teach me."

"I'll take you out this coming weekend. There's a resort on the other side where we'll have dinner and go dancing. Afterwards we'll sleep on the boat overnight."

"That sounds heavenly, but now I want to know what has produced those lines around that mouth I can't stop kissing."

He drew her over to the love seat and sat down with her, resting his arm on the frame behind her.

"As I told you when you first came to Vallefiore, our country has too much corruption causing serious trouble. My father did his best to deal with the problems. But just when he was gaining ground, he was stricken with Alzheimer's."

"I realize that's why you were so involved when you returned from England. But I had no idea how deeply you've had to contend with these problems."

"I'm glad you understand. The day Giovanni informed me you had arrived in Vallefiore, I'd been in one of the villages where I'd ordered some arrests. I had just left there to drive to Caserta, another village, to do an investigation. But when I knew you were at the hotel, I turned around and sped home."

He took a few minutes to explain the reason for the arrests. "But there are other problems cropping up. Because prosecutors have tried to break up certain strongholds, the criminals have been pushed back to their rural origins. Some of them have been operating their corrupt money laundering and drug business dealings here in Vallefiore for years.

"Let me give you an example of what has been happening on another part of our island. A family of wheat farmers have complained to the police that a huge herd of cows and horses have been invading their fields and destroying their entire wheat harvest."

"That's unconscionable, Enrico."

"Amen. Illegal grazing is the oldest form of intimidation. Six months ago a poisoned dog and half a dozen poisoned cow carcasses were delivered to the home of one of the farmers. A few months later the farmer's thresher had been destroyed."

She shook her head.

"All this has to be stopped, but it takes a lot of undercover investigating and difficult police infiltration work to produce the proof for the prosecutors. Since I've given our police full power to go after these people, we're getting a lot of pushback."

"You mean death threats." Donetta was a quick study. "Who's receiving them?"

"In the past, a police chief and several of the officials in my government."

"What about you?"

"I've had several. When Giovanni phoned me just now, he told me the latest threat against me personally came into the office by an anonymous phone call they couldn't trace. The timing coincides with those arrests I ordered in Avezzano on the day you flew here."

"I hope you've quadrupled the security surrounding you."

"Around all of us and now you. We've tried to shield my mother, but her palace spies keep her informed. If she brings any of this up during dinner, I wanted you to be prepared."

"Is this the news you didn't want to talk about when we left on our honeymoon?"

He nodded. "As you can see, I'm going to have my hands full cracking down on this criminal element. With you governing the normal areas of our government on a day-to-day basis from here on out, I'll be free to set up and follow through to trap these low-lifes and put them away for good."

"I know it's dangerous business, but if anyone can handle it and make a difference, you can."

"Thank heaven you have confidence in me. Tomorrow we'll go to my office and I'll walk you through my schedule of responsibilities, many of which you'll understand because you've been a close observer of your father all your life. There won't be anything you can't handle. I know in my gut you're going to be a great ruler."

She stared hard at him, as if mystified. "Why do you have so much faith in me?"

Because Giovanni had made him party to a very important secret and Enrico loved her enough to help her succeed at something she'd wanted all her life.

"I've observed your strength for years. You have a natural leadership ability along with a softness that sets you apart from everyone else. The way you've handled my mother so far has been masterful."

"In that case we'd better be on time."

His half smile melted her bones. "She

knows we're still on our honeymoon and will forgive us if we're a few minutes late."

"But she'll like me better if I don't find ways to detain you when she wants your attention."

He chuckled. "You're sounding like an intuitive queen already. When I first saw you astride your horse Luna, you sat like a young queen. I was mesmerized by a ten-year-old girl who had an astounding bearing and command of her horse.

"During the jumping, your composure was flawless. You weren't like any other girl, Donetta, and my impression of you never changed that you were someone exceptional. I couldn't wait to see you again at the next *concorso*, and the next."

Her gaze didn't leave his. "You've left me speechless."

He kissed her and they clung before he pulled her to her feet and they left to walk to the small dining room in the other part of the palace. This time his mother was already seated at the table next to his father, waiting for them. King Nuncio's casted lower arm was in a sling. His caregiver was helping him eat. Enrico's heart went out to him.

"Your Majesty." Donetta curtsied to him and then bowed to the queen. "Your Majesty, I'm so sorry His Majesty fell. How hard that must've been for him and you. We came back the minute we learned what had happened."

"You were away much longer than I had anticipated." Her wintry tone couldn't have been more deflating.

"You're only given one honeymoon in life, Mamma. We wanted to make it last as long as possible."

Enrico kissed his parents before seating Donetta next to him. The staff served them dinner and poured coffee. He waited until they'd left the dining room to talk.

"To be honest, we had the honeymoon of a lifetime and couldn't bear to come back."

The queen's eyes riveted on him were closer to black than brown. "At least you *came* back. There's been another death threat on your life, *figlio mio.*"

"Giovanni has already informed me, but it's nothing new."

"You're entirely too cavalier about it. When I learned the two of you have been camping out instead of flying to another

country, I couldn't believe you'd left your-
selves open as targets."

"I understand your fear, and I'm afraid
that's my fault," Donetta spoke up. "Enrico
asked me where I'd like to go. We share a lot
of the same interests and love being in the
mountains."

"But that's not the proper kind of honeymoon for you."

"It was what we both wanted, Mamma,
and we've never been so happy. Just so you
know, I'll be spending all day tomorrow and
evening with Donetta. If there's anything I
can do for you or Papà before morning, I'll
be happy to do it now."

"As a matter of fact there are several things
we need to discuss."

"I totally understand you two have missed
each other and want to talk," Donetta spoke
up. "I have some phone calls to make to my
sisters, so why don't I leave you now. We'll
see each other later, Enrico."

He loved this wife of his for her understanding. Giving her a kiss, he helped her
to her feet.

"Thank you for the lovely welcome-home
dinner, Your Majesty. *Buona notte.*"

Donetta sent her husband a silent message that she'd be waiting for him and then left to go back to his apartment. But some of their earlier conversation had given her the oddest feeling and she was anxious to talk it over with Fausta.

Once she reached the bedroom, she hung up her dress and brushed her teeth. After putting on a yellow cotton shorty nightgown, she sat up in the bed to talk to her.

Disappointed when her call went to voice mail, she left a message for her sister to phone her back when she could. Fausta was probably still out with Mia and her friends.

The next call to her sister Lanza went to voice mail, too. Donetta left the message that she and Enrico were back from their camping honeymoon and installed at the palace. She hoped to hear from her soon.

After sending her love, Donetta hung up and reached for the TV remote to watch the nightly news. She imagined Enrico would join his mother and talk to her while the caregiver put his father to bed. Enrico would probably be late returning to their apartment.

A half hour later, the phone rang. It was Fausta. "Thanks for calling me back."

"I've been hoping to hear from you. Is he still to die for?"

"Yes."

"Just yes? What kind of an answer is that?"

"I— It's an I-don't-know kind of answer," she said, her voice faltering.

"Donetta—what's wrong?"

She sucked in her breath. "Maybe nothing and I'm just being paranoid."

"About what?"

"Everything has been so divinely perfect until this afternoon."

"Go on."

"Today was the first time he talked about my running the country. He kept paying me all these compliments and telling me I was going to be a great leader. It sounded so odd when he doesn't know if I could do the job or not.

"When I asked him why he had such faith in me, he said that I'd seemed like a queen to him even when I was ten years old and he'd always admired my strength. Don't you find that strange? Bizarre even?"

"Are you kidding me? He's in love and letting you know how much! Before you got married, he said he wanted you to rule equally with him. How has that changed?"

"I don't know!" she cried. "You weren't there. Enrico was…different."

"Isn't this what you've always wanted? To be queen?"

Donetta gripped the phone tighter. "I thought I did once. But not like this…"

"Not like what?"

"What he said to me today didn't sound like the real Enrico. It was more like he was reading from a script. Oh—I realize I'm not explaining this right or making sense. All I know is, he didn't seem like the man I married. When he told me I'd been a close observer of my father all my life and there wouldn't be anything I couldn't handle, it disturbed me."

"Disturbed you? Am I talking to the real Donetta?"

"Don't make fun of me, Fausta."

"I'm not. I'm just surprised."

"Why does he think he knows so much about me? Something else is strange, too. He was supposed to be crowned king at his marriage, but because he married me instead of Valentina, his mother wouldn't allow the coronation to happen."

"You're kidding. I thought his father was incapacitated. Is Enrico upset about it?"

"I can't tell." Suddenly she heard a noise and knew Enrico had come back. "I'll have to call you another time, Fausta. Good night." She clicked off and put the phone on the side table just as he walked into the room. Thankfully, the TV was still on.

Those penetrating black eyes of his zeroed in on her. "There you are. Just where I want you to be and looking delightful in yellow." When he disappeared into the bathroom, she turned the TV off with the remote.

In a minute he'd changed out of his clothes and put on a robe. After turning out the lights, he slid into bed and pulled her against him. "Our first night in our own home. I hope it will feel that way to you soon."

"I'm with you forever. It's all that matters."

It *was* all that mattered.

Fausta had been right about Enrico wanting to show her how much he loved and believed in her. Donetta had been reading way too much into the earlier conversation with her husband. She loved him more than life itself. "Is your mother all right?" She kissed his hard jaw.

"No," he said honestly. "She can't let it go that I didn't marry Valentina, but in time she'll come around. You're wonderful to her. Please don't let her upset you too much. The day will come when she'll learn to love you."

"I want to believe that, too. Now tell me what else is wrong."

She heard his sharp intake of breath. "The truth is, she's afraid I'm going to be assassinated."

Donetta's fingers tightened in his hair. "You can't blame her for that. I think deep down that the wives and children of any sovereign harbor that same fear. If you want to know the truth, my sisters and I have always lived under that same worry where our father is concerned."

"But you can handle it."

Enrico was wrong. The thought of losing him to a sniper's bullet or the slash of a dagger terrified her.

He held her tighter. "The problem is, she's demanding I stop taking on the corrupt elements with so much force. Of course that's something I won't do."

"Doesn't she realize you're carrying out the same policies as your father?"

"Yes and no. In the last year I've been more aggressive than he ever was. These death threats prove I'm getting more results with every arrest. The progress we're making is vital for our country's welfare. My goal is to rid Vallefiore of this menace.

"Since college Giovanni has been helping me develop a massive internal structure of intelligence operatives. In time we're going to win this war. We can't back down now."

Donetta rose up on one elbow. "*That's* the reason she didn't allow the coronation to happen. Once you become king, with all the power, you'll be their target more than ever, and she's terrified of losing you."

"Trust my brilliant wife to figure it out, but we have the needed kind of security in place to ensure that you and I will reign for a long time, God willing."

They *were* in God's hands. She knew that.

CHAPTER NINE

"I ADMIRE YOU for your fearlessness and determination, Enrico. I promise I'll do everything I can to help."

"You already do that just being here in my arms."

The time for talk was over. With one kiss he swept her away. They gave in to their desire, which continued to grow with every passing minute, taking them far into the night. Donetta fell asleep nestled against him.

They slept in and enjoyed breakfast in the apartment. After both of them dressed in casual clothes, they left for the wing of the palace that housed the government. His staff resembled a small city of men and women officials.

When they saw Enrico, they all stood and clapped. Chief among them was Giovanni.

His arms were folded. He wore a broad smile on his good-looking face.

Her husband put his arm around her waist. "Thank you for welcoming us this morning. Let me introduce you to my bride, Princess Donetta Rossiano of Domodossola. She will be working with all of us from here on out on a daily basis.

"You are to offer Her Highness the same help and courtesy you offer me. There will be times when I'll be away on other business, but she will be here. Any matters that would come to me will now come to her. Let me make it clear that she'll speak with the same authority as I do."

Donetta marveled how quickly he was changing the dynamics of a system of male succession that had been in place for centuries. Already Enrico was preparing the staff for her to carry out the role he'd created for her.

Everyone continued to pay attention, but deep down she knew they didn't really believe he meant every word of that speech. But in time they'd find out and be in shock. Common sense told her they weren't going to like it.

He ushered her through massive, ornate floor-to-ceiling doors into his large, sumptuous office, where the king had worked until he'd become incapacitated. A framed picture of Enrico's father hung on the wall.

A stand placed in one corner held the flag of Vallefiore and the individual flags of each province. There was also a grouping of leather couches and chairs around an octagonal coffee table with a fabulous Moorish pot overflowing with flowers.

Enrico pulled out his swivel armchair for her to be seated at his desk. He perched his hard-muscled body on a corner of the massive oak desk and buzzed one of the secretaries in the outer office. He asked that another matching chair, desk and lamp be brought in by the end of the day.

With that accomplished, he flashed his devastating smile that sent her heartbeat skyrocketing. "Your Highness? Behold your kingdom. All that I have is yours."

Overcome by his generous heart, she felt her eyes prickle with salty tears. "Are you sure this is what you want?"

"Aren't you?"

He often answered a question with another

198 THE PRINCE'S FORBIDDEN BRIDE

one. This question gave her pause. As she was growing up, she'd always wanted to be queen by right of succession. At least that was what she'd told herself. But in time she could see that it had been nothing more than a child's pipe dream.

For Enrico to walk in here today and install her as a fait accompli in front of his subjects who answered to a king and no one else was an entirely different proposition.

For one thing, Enrico hadn't been crowned king officially yet. If his mother continued to feel so negatively over his choice of wife, maybe it wouldn't happen for several more years.

Donetta wasn't Enrico's queen in the legal sense that he could set her on the throne beside him. No matter what he'd promised her, for the time being she was Princess Donetta, wife of the crown prince. But she'd promised to help him and she would do everything in her power because she adored him.

"I'm ready to learn."

"I'm glad, because there's no time to waste. The first thing to do is get on the computer and we'll go over my daily routine. Later on, we'll take a look at my weekly and monthly agenda."

Finally she could see the world he'd been immersed in since college. He carried a huge load.

"In a minute I'll show you the list of our legislators, the cabinet and staff overseeing the military, housing and education, with names, phone numbers and job descriptions. However, the names of your bodyguards and mine won't be on any computer."

Of course not. Her father had security, but she couldn't remember him ever having to deal with a personal death threat.

"Another file will show you the entire floor plan and layout of the palace, plus the palace staff. We also run many businesses and some hospitals and organizations in the city and throughout the country. I'll show you how to access that list as well."

Donetta knew she'd be looking at it a lot until she had everything memorized.

"Giovanni is the head of security and that includes the country's police and fire departments. He also runs our Sanfratellano Horse Federation and will familiarize you with everything when you're ready. My sisters oversee many charities and will be available to you. Soon I'll discuss our treaties and immigration policies with you."

By midafternoon Donetta's head was too full of new information to learn any more and Enrico knew it. "We've done enough for today, *bellissima*. Let's eat lunch in our apartment, and then I have a surprise for you."

"You do too much for me."

"I'll never be able to do enough."

As they started to leave, Giovanni knocked before coming in. "Excuse me, Donetta. Can I talk to your husband for a minute?"

"You can," Donetta said with a smile. "I'll see you at the apartment, Enrico. Shall I call down to the kitchen?"

He nodded. "All you have to do is pick up the phone and give the order."

She walked down the hallway lined with glassed-in offices. Many curious eyes followed her progress. Not all looked that friendly and she understood why, but maybe she was letting her paranoia take over again. Donetta couldn't afford for that to happen.

Giovanni closed the door so no one could see or hear them. "When you introduced Donetta to everyone this morning, the part about her having the same power as you didn't go over well with anyone, especially you know who."

Enrico nodded. "Leopold. The man can't be trusted, but father appointed him to the cabinet and he's a good friend of Mamma's."

"Not to mention a titled member of the aristocracy. I saw him get on the phone immediately."

"That's no surprise, but the only way to make this change was to deal with it head on."

"You certainly did that," his cousin murmured. "I just wanted to give you a heads-up."

He clasped Giovanni's shoulder. "No one ever had a better friend."

"How's it going with Donetta?"

"I didn't know I could be this happy. This afternoon I'm giving her my wedding present."

"Does she know?"

"Not yet. How's the woman situation with you? Are you still seeing Celesta?"

"No. That's over."

"You sound like the old me. One of these days it'll be your turn, cousin."

"You think?"

"I know."

On his way out of the office he talked to several associates and then hurried to his apartment. He found Donetta on the phone with her sister. A minute later their lunch arrived and he carried the tray to the dining room table so they could eat.

She followed him and he helped her to sit. They were both hungry. "How are your parents?"

"Amazingly well. The news of Lanza's pregnancy seems to have given them a new lease on life."

"Don't you think that seeing you happy has made a difference, too?"

"Of course. They like you very much already."

"That's nice to hear." The baked cod with green beans and potatoes hit the spot. "Just think how thrilled they'll be when we can tell them the news that we're expecting our own baby."

She finished her coffee. "That's my greatest wish."

"And mine. In the meantime, let's take a short drive to the other end of the property.

Everything is open to the public except the tennis courts and swimming pool."

Enrico had told her he had a surprise for her. Donetta had seen the map that showed the twelve-square-mile Montedoro estate. She was excited as they left the palace in his Jaguar. He drove them along a road behind the palace.

"The estate gardens are breathtaking."

"Mamma oversees their care and design. Every day she pushes Papà for a walk along the paths. She's an amazing gardener."

"I'd love to learn from her."

Soon she saw a cluster of buildings in the distance, among them a state-of-the-art stable that could probably house a dozen horses. She turned her head to look at him. *"Enrico?"*

"I see you've already guessed my surprise," he teased.

When he parked in front, she was out of the car in a flash. He caught up to her and took her inside to the fourth stall. Her eyes clapped on a gorgeous dark chocolate brown mare.

"My precious wife, meet Mahbouba. It means beloved in Arabic."

"I can't tell you what this means to me," she whispered and threw her arms around him. "Ever since you told me about the Sanfratellano horses, I've dreamed of owning one. In fact when I came for your *concorso*, I'd planned to arrange to buy one. But everything changed after our campout. I knew I couldn't trust myself to be with you any longer. She's really mine?"

"All yours."

Donetta approached her horse, talking softly to her while she rubbed her head and neck. The mare seemed to like the attention while Donetta inspected her legs and hooves. "You're beautiful, Mahbouba." She looked over at Enrico. "Can we go riding?"

"Let's go bareback. She's been broken in. I asked the trainer to get her ready for us. After I help you mount, we'll walk back to the end of the stable to get my stallion Quatan."

"Every day with you is a miracle."

She pressed a kiss to her husband's lips before he helped her on and handed her the reins. The mare pranced in place while Donetta let her get used to her weight. "Come on," she said in soothing tones. "Let's go for a ride."

Enrico started walking. Donetta directed the mare to follow him. It had been over a month since she'd ridden, and now she felt euphoric. When they reached his stallion's stall, both horses neighed. Enrico moved inside and mounted his steed with his usual masculine dexterity.

"That new black stallion is a prize. He's gorgeous."

"I didn't think I could replace Rajah, but Quatan is exceptional." He made a clicking sound and headed out of the stable to the field. Donetta was close behind, taking care not to startle the mare until she got used to her.

All the while they walked, she talked to her and patted her neck. "You're a real beauty. Did you know I saw your brothers and sisters running across the plain? I hope you don't miss them too much."

Enrico must have heard her. His smile lit up her universe. "Keep that up and you'll have her eating out of your hand before the day is out."

They walked for a good half hour and then returned to the stable. When they came to Mahbouba's stall, Donetta slid off to give her water and feed her. Then she reached for the currycomb hanging on a hook to brush her down. Enrico stalled his horse and came back to watch her.

Donetta turned to him. "She's as good as gold."

"So you think you'll keep her?"

She laughed. "This morning you presented your kingdom to me. Now you've presented me with this beautiful animal. You make me too happy." Her voice caught.

"We'll go riding every day, either morning or evening, and get you a saddle you can break in."

After giving her mare more love, they left the stable and got back in his car. As he drove them to the palace, she finally had an idea for a wedding present she could give him. Right away she would secretly find out the name of the artist who'd done Rajah's picture in oils. If he or she were available, Donetta would commission a painting of Quatan and have it hung on the wall of their bedroom.

But she wanted to do something for him right now. When they arrived and hurried to the apartment, she turned to him. "I'm going to cook our dinner tonight."

"I'm already salivating."

"Will it be all right if I call the kitchen for the ingredients I need?"

"Go ahead while I check my messages."

A half hour later they'd both showered and gotten comfortable in their robes while she cooked up a storm. Donetta ordered some red wine to go with their meal.

"I'll feed you." She stood next to him and gave him a heaping forkful of fried bruschetta.

He munched on it before reaching for her. "I've died and gone to heaven."

She chuckled. "I hope you'll like my *escalope de veau* with rice just as much."

Enrico devoured their meal in no time. "Promise me you'll cook our dinner every night."

They clinked their glasses of wine. "I plan to do whatever you want to keep you satisfied."

When they'd finished, he turned on the radio to some music and took her out on the patio off the dining room to dance with her. Their dance soon moved to the bedroom just as his cell phone rang.

"We're not home," he said aloud.

"You need to pick up," she urged.

"I'm still on my honeymoon, *esposa mia*."

"But it might be important."

"You're right, but I resent the intrusion." He reached for his phone before looking at her in surprise. "It's Lia."

Donetta got in bed and listened, but she only heard half of the conversation. Before long he turned to her with an almost forbidding expression.

"She's been with mother for the last two hours. Mamma's informant told her about my speech this morning. She's not only livid, but she called an emergency meeting of the most influential members of my cabinet."

Donetta got out of bed. "Why would she do such a thing?"

"She's asked them to gather the entire legislature in the next twenty-four hours for an emergency meeting. She's demanding they call for a vote that will bar you legally from having anything to do with my work as crown prince."

"Oh, no—" A shiver racked Donetta's body. "You warned me she would fight it, but to talk to your ministers behind your back…"

"Mamma has gone too far. I'm stymied by

her behavior. It simply isn't like her to make this so ugly. Something's going on I don't know about. I've got to talk to Giovanni and find out what he knows."

"Wait, Enrico. You and I need to talk first. Before you do anything, I think you should go to your mother tonight and work things out with her even if it takes all night. This situation on top of her disappointment over Valentina has been too much for her."

Lines marred his handsome features. "I'm too upset to talk to her right now."

"But she's more upset than you and we know why. She's frightened for your life and is threatened by my presence. I'm sure she believes I'm influencing you to do things you would never do if you hadn't met me."

He shook his dark head. "She has no right to be this cruel to you."

"I agree. You warned me she would be difficult, but I didn't want to believe you. I don't understand it when she loves you so much. I'm positive she doesn't believe I'm worthy of you. Let's face it. She's not ready for a daughter-in-law like me. I'm a horsey person who loves to camp out. I arrived on your doorstep and upset her world in one day.

"Instead of a big wedding in the cathedral in front of your countrymen, we married quietly without anyone knowing. Her world has spun out of control. In her mind I'm a terrible person and the cause of her pain.

"You need to spend time with her and listen to her fears. She didn't know you and I have had a long history. It has shaken her. If she understood more, she'd see why we wanted to get married immediately.

"Help her understand that you'd like to be able to concentrate on the threat to your country if you're going to make a real difference. Let her see that you would like the woman you married and trust to run the daily affairs while you deal with the criminal elements. She has no idea how much I'd love to help you in any way I can. For both our sakes, please go to her tonight and explain. I'm begging you."

At first she didn't think she was getting through to him. But he eventually got up from the bed and started to get dressed. "I'll go, but I might not be back until morning. Besides talking to her, I've got phone calls to make. Don't wait up for me. I'm so sorry, Donetta."

"Don't worry about me, darling. You're the only person in the world who can fix this."

"I intend to," he ground out. "She had no right to hurt you this way. You're my wife!" he exploded in a savage voice.

"I'm not the one hurt," she cried even though she was dying inside. But for the first time since she'd flown in to Vallefiore, he wasn't listening. In the next breath he left the bedroom without holding or kissing her first. For him to do that revealed the depth of his torment.

No sooner had he gone than the landline phone rang. Donetta threw on her robe and rushed over to pick it up. "This is Donetta."

"Oh, Donetta. It's Lia. I'm so glad you answered. Are you alone?"

"Yes. Enrico has gone to talk to your mother."

"That's good, because I need to talk to you. Can I come to your apartment? I should be there in five minutes."

"Of course. I'll be right here waiting."

Donetta hung up and paced the living room floor until she heard a knock on the outer door.

"Come in, Lia."

"Forgive me for barging in, but I can't keep this to myself." Enrico's sister hurried inside and sat down on one of the couches, patting a spot so Donetta would sit by her.

"What's wrong?"

"I overheard my mother talking to our cabinet leader, Leopold, earlier in the small salon. She's talking about having your marriage annulled because it wasn't legal under our constitution. I don't know if she can really do that, but she's going to try to influence them. Out of respect for our father, they'll probably listen to her. If that doesn't work, then she wants Leo to begin divorce proceedings for the two of you."

Donetta got up from the couch. "Enrico warned me she wouldn't want our marriage, but I never dreamed it could get this bad."

"Mamma has surprised me, too. I heard her say it's not too late because she knows Valentina will still marry him if he can be free. Since the whole world doesn't know about it yet, she's hoping your marriage can be undone and go away. But it has to happen right away."

"Oh, Lia. I don't know what to do."

"I wish I knew how to help you and my

mother. I'm sure she's talking about a divorce with Enrico right now in the salon. I've never seen her in such a rage. This is so awful, because I think you and Enrico are perfect for each other."

Donetta's heart warmed to her new sister-in-law. "Thank you for saying that and defending us." She leaned over to give her a hug. "I owe you a debt of gratitude for everything, especially for that wedding dress and all the lovely things that went with it. You're wonderful."

"So are you. Enrico has never been so happy. I wish there were something I could do to calm my mother, but she's not listening to reason right now and Papà's fall didn't help."

"I agree she has more on her plate than a human should have to handle. I know deep down she's a wonderful person or she wouldn't have such marvelous children like Enrico and you girls. You don't know how much I appreciate your coming here to warn me. When Enrico comes back, I'll be prepared."

Lia nodded. "I'd better leave so he doesn't find me here."

"He said he'd probably be gone all night." Donetta followed her to the door. "We'll stay in close touch. Thank you again for being such a good friend to us."

After another hug, Lia hurried off. Donetta watched until she disappeared, but she couldn't stand to wait for Enrico. With no time to spare she left the apartment and hurried through the palace to the salon to find her husband. But as she approached the door, she heard his mother's voice. "It's better that she leave the country, Enrico. You shouldn't have married her in the first place."

Pierced to the heart with pain, that was all Donetta needed to hear. Once alone in the apartment again, she knew what she had to do. She refused to stand in Enrico's way. He must go on to be king. The country needed him. Though she would have loved to get behind him and manage by his side, it was better that he get the chance to rule, even if it meant she couldn't remain his wife.

Her beloved husband needed help. The one path open to her was to leave the country and give him the chance to handle this desperate situation without her. It was the only way he could take on the throne.

When she found her phone, she called the pilot of the Rossiano royal jet. Donetta asked him to fly to Vallefiore ASAP. She would be waiting on the tarmac.

At three in the morning, she slipped out of the apartment with her two suitcases, praying Enrico wouldn't catch her in the act of flee-ing. The palace guard saw her leave in the taxi she'd called for. But she knew that by the time he would have reported her actions and someone tracked down Enrico to tell him, she'd be on her way to Domodossola.

So far, so good, she thought as she boarded the jet and they took off. She sat there during the flight absolutely devastated for Enrico and the trouble his mother was creating. In hindsight she realized that what he'd wanted just wasn't possible. His mother had lived a lifetime with her own set of principles and couldn't change now.

Donetta refused to hold him or his king-dom back by her selfishness. She wouldn't fight a divorce. All she could do was return home and help her own family.

Oh, Enrico... I love you so much.

An hour and a half later the plane landed. Enrico hadn't phoned her yet. Maybe he still hadn't heard that she'd left the palace. Hoping that he didn't have to cope with that worry yet, she undid her seat belt and phoned Fausta.

"You've left Enrico?" Fausta sounded aghast.

"It's not what you think. Can you come for me in the limo so we can talk?" It was six in the morning. "I don't dare phone the parents. They need their sleep." The last thing she wanted to do was bring them more grief, but under the circumstances she was afraid it was going to be inevitable.

"I agree. I'll be there within half an hour."

"Bless you."

CHAPTER TEN

AFTER LEAVING HIS parents' apartment, Enrico raced to his in the other part of the palace. He needed to talk to Donetta. On his way, he got a phone call from his cousin. He clicked on, trying to keep his emotions under control after the long, disturbing talk with his mother and Leopold.

"Giovanni? I presume you know everything."

"I'm afraid I know more than you do."

"What do you mean?"

"The guard outside the entrance to your wing of the palace phoned to let me know Donetta left the palace in the middle of the night in a taxi."

No! His body broke out in a cold sweat.

"Her bodyguards followed her to the airport and confirmed she flew out on the royal jet from Domodossola. I contacted their country's police to put a bodyguard on her the moment she landed. A few minutes ago they confirmed that she had arrived and was picked up by Princess Fausta, who also has security."

Enrico reeled. That was all he needed to hear. "Thank you for all you've done. I should never have left her while I tried to talk sense to Leopold and Mamma. It accomplished nothing."

"Hold on. I'm coming to your apartment now so we can talk without anyone listening in on our phone conversation."

By the time his cousin burst into the apartment, Enrico was in agony. The two stared at each other.

"I should never have told Donetta she could share the throne with me, Giovanni. After what I learned tonight, Leo said that the leaders of the cabinet would give me a no-confidence vote if I had her rule with me. It could be the end of my rule, too, and throw our country into utter chaos."

"You'll have to listen to them, Enrico. Our country needs you at the helm. The problem is, they're not ready for a modern world."

"Apparently not. It isn't as if I'd proposed changing the rules of succession!"

"The problem is, no wife of a sovereign of Vallefiore has ever shared the throne. It's never been done."

"Then something needs to change, Giovanni. We no longer live in the age of dinosaurs."

"Not changing the rules has kept the monarchy strong."

"So strong that the cabinet's rejection and Mamma's have done irreparable personal damage to my wife. Mamma's insisting on a divorce, which is out of the question. Donetta married me after I made her the promise that she would rule as queen in her own right.

"It's something she's wanted all her life. I thought I could make her dream a reality. As your informant once told you, Donetta stayed single all these years because she wanted to change the laws of Domodossola and be queen.

"When she realized she could never do away with the rules of succession in her country, she grabbed the chance I offered her. I believed I could work a miracle. Donetta trusted me enough that she walked out on Arnaud because of what I could do for her.

"I have to be honest with myself. It may have not been a lie, but my marriage proposal was made on shaky ground and now I'm paying for it. But I'm not about to lose her, because I love her too much. I told Mamma I would never divorce her."

"How can I help?"

"Giovanni, will you fly to Domodossola right now in the jet and bring her back? I know how her mind works. She'll tell me she'll agree to a divorce. Say whatever you have to in order to bring her back with you."

"I'm on my way, but don't you want to go?"

"I can't if I'm going to get everything ready in time. I've made plans that I pray will convince her I can't live without her. When you reach the airport, drive her as far as the road leading down to the waterfall where we had our honeymoon."

"Good news, cousin. The tent is still there, being guarded. I haven't had time to see about dismantling it yet. Now I'm glad I haven't."

"That makes two of us. I'll be there waiting."

"Now you're talking."

"When this is over, I'm going to repay you for being the best friend a man could ever hope to have and give you the long vacation you deserve and anything else your heart desires."

When the limo reached the palace, Fausta asked the driver to take her around to the side entrance closest to her apartment. Donetta hurried inside with her and they closeted themselves in her bedroom. Before long their parents would hear that Donetta had arrived, but for the time being they were free to talk.

She checked her phone. By now Enrico had to know she'd flown here, but he hadn't phoned or texted her yet. Still, it was early in the day. All she could do was hope that by her leaving Vallefiore, he'd be free to do what he had to do as crown prince.

"Sit down and talk to me, Donetta. Was it really so terrible with his mother?"

"You can't imagine. She was unfriendly the first time I was introduced to her at the *concorso.* It grew worse from that time on. After Lia told me about his talk with her last night, I had to leave.

"I was afraid that the very sight of me was too much for his mother to handle. She was taken by surprise from the very beginning. I love Enrico so terribly and can't bear it that I've come between them."

"From what you've told me, she was already upset because he never wanted to marry Valentina."

"The whole thing's a nightmare, Fausta. I'll give him a divorce if that's what is needed." While Donetta stood there with tears gushing down her cheeks, her cell phone rang. "Maybe that's Enrico—"

She pulled it out of her purse and checked the caller ID. "It's Giovanni. At least *he's* calling me."

Fausta watched her as she answered. "Put it on speaker."

Donetta nodded. "Giovanni?"

"Can you talk?" He sounded so anxious her heart plunged to the floor.

"Yes! I guess you know I just arrived here in Domodossola. My sister Fausta is with me.

Is Enrico all right? I love him so much and have been hoping, waiting for him to call."

She heard him expel a deep sigh. "I have a better idea. I'm on my way in the jet right now to bring you back on Enrico's orders. Then you can talk to him yourself. Be at the airport in an hour."

"But Giovanni—"

"There's no time to talk."

She heard the click and looked at Fausta.

Her sister was smiling. "You ran out on your husband and it didn't fix anything. Now he's searching for you. If I were you, I'd take a quick shower, grab a bite to eat and let me drive you back to the airport with your bags."

"I'm frightened, Fausta."

"Have a little faith, sister. I'm afraid if you don't show up with Giovanni, your husband will send reinforcements and it could get uglier than even *you* dreamed."

Enrico checked his watch. Eleven o'clock in the morning. He'd arrived at the camp behind the guys who'd trailed the horses and would take care of them. He waited on his stallion for the sight of Giovanni's car on the mountain road.

Donetta's saddled mare stood next to them with the reins in Enrico's hands. After Donetta arrived, they would ride down to the camp together. It would give him the chance he needed to tell her he would choose her above his kingdom. She was all he wanted.

Earlier this morning, with the help of his sisters, he'd prevailed on his mother to accept his marriage to Donetta, but there'd be no more talk of her ruling equally with him. In his heart Enrico planned that one day he could give Donetta the prize she'd always hoped for. That time would come.

His heart leaped when he saw the blue car round the bend. Giovanni pulled up to the side of the road where Enrico was waiting. Donetta got out of the car. The first thing he saw were those shimmering light green eyes clapped on him in stunned surprise.

"I don't blame you for wanting to run away, *amata*. Thank heaven you came back." He waved to Giovanni, who reciprocated before returning to the city. "Mahbouba is waiting for you."

"I can't believe you're here. Giovanni was so mysterious about where we were going."

"My cousin was only carrying out my

wishes. I couldn't believe it when you weren't in our apartment earlier, but all our troubles are over now. Let's ride."

Enrico watched her mount with a grace that was thrilling to watch. They started to make their way through the trees. "Tell me something, *bellissima.* Why didn't you wait for me?"

His question stunned her. "Surely you must know! I wanted to ease the tension with your mother and decided that getting away from the palace was the only thing to do. I've come between you and her in the most terrible way possible and thought it best to give you the space to work things out with her."

A groan came out of him. "Lia told me what she told you. Don't you know I couldn't handle it if you ever left me?"

"But your mother despises me."

"My mother isn't your problem, Donetta. Our marriage is all we need to worry about."

She gripped the reins so tight it hurt her hand. "That's not true. She's been hurt so badly it's killing me."

"I think we're talking at cross-purposes here."

Donetta frowned. "I don't understand what you're saying."

"Answer me one question. *Why* did you marry me?"

"Do you really have to ask me that?" she cried.

"Just tell me."

"Because I loved you from the moment we met years ago. When you told me you were planning to get married, too, and then admitted that I was the woman, I almost died from happiness."

"So it didn't have anything to do with my telling you that I would make you queen in your own right after we were married?"

What? "Of course it didn't! I wanted to be your wife, period! That's the *only* reason I flew here the next day! Why would you say such a thing?"

"Because a friend of Giovanni's, who happens to be friend of your sister Fausta's, told him that you never intended to marry. He said it was because you wanted to be queen of Domodossola one day and didn't want a husband."

Donetta let out a cry. "It wouldn't have been Mia Giancarlo, would it?"

"She's the one. After I saw you in Madrid, I told my cousin I was in love with you and wanted to marry you. He told me I was out of luck. He said that the only reason you were still single was because you wanted to be queen in your own right. You didn't want a husband. When I heard that, I loved you so much I didn't let that stop me and I vowed to find a way to get you to marry me."

Right now Donetta's heart was pounding so hard it actually hurt. "*That's* why you told me you would make me queen?"

"The *only* reason! But when I invited you to Vallefiore and you said you were going to marry Arnaud, I was devastated. Still, I refused to give up. When you were getting on the jet to fly home, I gave it one last stab, hoping you would be persuaded to marry me and not leave."

"I almost didn't!" she cried.

"After you flew off, I never dreamed you'd change your mind. I'm surprised I didn't go into cardiac arrest when Giovanni phoned and told me you'd returned to Vallefiore."

"Oh, Enrico—" Now she understood why he'd talked about what a great leader she would make. Fausta had been right. Enrico had been saying everything he could to show her he loved her!

"Tell me the truth, *amata*. Are you hurt because I can't make you a queen after all?"

They'd reached the camp. Donetta jumped off her horse and tied it to a tree before wheeling around. She looked at Enrico, who'd started to dismount.

"I gave up the dream of being a queen a long time ago. It was a foolish, stupid, unrealistic idea I developed as a girl that could never have happened. When you told me I could reign equally with you, I had trouble believing it. But I was so thrilled you wanted to marry me that I was happy to do anything I could to help you, if that's what you wanted."

Enrico let out a groan and hurried over to her, wrapping her in his arms. "This whole misunderstanding is my fault for believing the gossip about you, Donetta."

She shook her head. "If anyone is to blame, it's I. Fausta grew up with me and knew my feelings when I was young. She didn't mean to tell Mia. I'm the one who should never have said anything so foolish.

"But Mia has a brother who had a crush on

me and knew I'd never give him the time of day. I know that's why she told her brother about my vow so he'd stop hoping for a chance with me."

"Donetta—" The revelations were flying fast and furious. "This news changes everything." He kissed her every feature. "Do you hear me, my love?"

"Yes. Oh, yes! But, darling, your mother needs to know that I've never tried to manipulate you. The only thing I plan to do is love you and our babies, if we're so lucky to have them. If she'll let me, I'll love her, too."

"You'll win her over, Donetta. I know you will."

"When I tell my parents that you tried to make my childhood dream come true, they'll love you all the more. But no one could love you the way I do. It's not possible."

Once again he picked her up in his arms and carried her inside the tent. For the next two hours they tried without success to assuage their desire, renewing their vows in the most elemental way.

He pulled her on top of him. "Promise me you'll never leave me again."

"I promise."

"Much as I want to have another long honeymoon with you, we need to get back to the palace. Mamma needs to know we have a solid marriage and nothing will hurt us."

"I love you so much, Enrico, and need to let her know how I feel."

Two hours later they were back in their apartment at the palace where she could shower and change into her pink suit. She wanted to look her best for Queen Teodora.

Enrico had arranged for them and Giovanni to eat an early dinner in the small dining room. He felt that the element of surprise when the three of them showed up would work in their favor.

The queen was already seated at the table, dressed in a lovely blue suit. Her dark brown eyes flashed in anger when she saw Donetta and Giovanni enter the room at Enrico's side. There was no sign of the king.

"Your Majesty." Donetta curtsied before Enrico helped her to a seat around the other side. "Is the king not well today?"

"He's never well and doesn't have his dinner until later."

"Zia Teodora?" Giovanni began. "We have

something of vital importance to share with you. So does Princess Donetta."

Her jaw hardened. "I heard you'd flown to Domodossola during the night."

"I did."

"But I brought her back on the royal jet," Giovanni explained. "The drastic situation required drastic measures in order to restore peace and understanding."

Donetta was holding her breath. Enrico gripped her hand.

"Thank you for accommodating us, Zia. What I have to tell you will change your perspective on everything."

After they were served dinner and coffee, Giovanni began. "My story starts when Enrico confided that he'd been in love with Donetta ever since their first *concorso* in England seventeen years ago. He kept his secret until we came home from Madrid about six weeks ago. That's the first time I'd heard that he'd been wanting to marry her since college. But I'm afraid I said something to him that presented a challenge."

In the next instant Donetta listened while Giovanni laid everything out for his aunt so there could be no misunderstanding. "When

232   THE PRINCE'S FORBIDDEN BRIDE

Enrico made his speech to the cabinet, he was fulfilling his promise to Donetta, who never wanted to rule equally with him."

The queen's expression underwent a fundamental change. "I still don't understand."

Donetta broke in and told her about her childhood dream to be queen of Domodossola one day. "My sister knew how I felt and shared it with her friend, who happens to be a friend of Giovanni's."

He nodded. "I told Enrico he would never be able to marry Donetta because she didn't intend to marry. She wanted to be queen in her own right."

"It was a ridiculous, foolish dream I gave up on a long time ago," Donetta explained. "When Arnaud pursued me and wanted to marry me, I knew I didn't love him. But if we had children, I knew it would bring me happiness. The trouble was, I had always loved Enrico and had waited in vain for a proposal from him."

Enrico spoke up. "When she came to our *concorso*, she let me know she planned to go home and tell Arnaud she would marry him. I proposed anyway. To influence her even more, I told her she could rule equally with me. Until this morning when I told her the truth, Donetta had no idea I had ever heard the gossip about her."

"You can't imagine my joy that Enrico loved me, Your Majesty," Donetta cried. "I told Arnaud it was over with us. Even if Enrico changed his mind about me, I knew I would never love anyone but him."

The queen sat back in the chair, her eyes dim with thoughts. "This explains why you could never get interested in Valentina, my son. What I don't understand is why you didn't tell me and your father."

Donetta broke in. "I didn't tell my parents about him, either. I would have if he'd kept on writing and wanted to see me. But there was never a word. My sister Fausta knew how I felt, but she never said anything."

Enrico's mother looked at her with sadness. "My husband was struggling so much at the time. When Enrico came home and took over, it was like a godsend. I can see now that I leaned on him too much and had too many expectations that didn't give him any free time."

Donetta smiled at her. "I just want you to know that I would have done whatever he asked. But now that I know everything, I have no plan to run the government with him, even if you and the cabinet were to allow it. Please convey that message to them.

"The truth is, I'm just so happy to be Enrico's wife that it's all I want, except to hope that one day you will learn to accept me a little bit. He loves you and his father more than you know."

The queen sat straighter in her chair. "It's very evident he's found the love of his life. I hope that one day you'll be able to forgive me for the ungracious way I have treated you."

Donetta felt her eyes smart. "There's nothing to forgive. My biggest worry is that Enrico will not forgive me for leaving."

"You know I have." Enrico kissed her cheek. "And my gratitude to Giovanni for helping us knows no bounds."

Queen Teodora patted Giovanni's arm. "He's my second son and I love him like my own. When his parents lost their lives in a plane accident, he became one of the family and has been a blessing."

Donetta smiled. "I can believe that. I love him, too."

After they'd finished their meal, Enrico

got up and walked over to his mother. "Why don't we go check on Papà?"

"I'd like that."

"Donetta? I'll see you back at our apartment in a little while."

"Take all the time you need." Both Giovanni and Donetta got to their feet. "Thank you for letting me talk to you, Your Majesty."

The queen actually smiled at her. "Call me Mamma."

Donetta left the dining room with Giovanni, who looked over at her. "I hope you realize my aunt just welcomed you to the family."

She nodded. "I'm still overcome that she has forgiven me."

"Beneath that exterior she has a heart of gold. But where Valentina was concerned, she had a soft spot. However, I'm afraid the princess no longer holds first place in her heart."

Donetta smiled at him. "Have you ever been interested in Valentina?"

"No, but there is one woman I've had my eye on for a couple of years. It's hopeless, of course."

"How can you say that?"

"Because it's your sister."

"Fausta?" she cried out in surprise.

"I met her in Paris. But I gave up on pursuing her when I heard the gossip about her." He flashed Donetta a glance. "Is it possible that by now she has given up the dream of marrying a commoner?"

What she'd give to have Giovanni for a brother-in-law! "I'm afraid not, or I'd throw her at you." He laughed that rich laugh, sounding so much like Enrico her heart hurt. "We're going to have to find you a woman you can't live without."

"Please do."

It was her turn to laugh.

"Do you know my cousin went through a period where he wished he hadn't been born royal? He eventually got over it."

"He told me about that. Would it surprise you to know my brother-in-law Stefano disliked being royal and was legally exempt for a decade? But that changed when his brother died and he married Lanza."

"Are they happy?"

"Ecstatic. But Fausta is different. She likes being royal and believes that if she marries a commoner, they'll have such an unusual, interesting marriage they'll always be in love. It's that unknown element separating the classes she believes is missing from many marriages, royal or otherwise."

"Her mind is as fascinating as yours."

"Mine doesn't match hers. When we were little, Mamma would read fairy tales to us. After she turned out the light and left the room, the three of us would discuss them for hours.

"Lanza loved *Cinderella* the most, where life would be perfect. Fausta loved *The Twelve Dancing Princesses*. She would speculate that instead of meeting a dumb prince, she would meet a commoner, which was much more exciting and dangerous."

He laughed. "What was your favorite?"

"I didn't have one because something was missing in all of them. So I wrote my own about a good queen who ran her country beautifully without any help."

"You're an original, Donetta Rossiano. So is Enrico."

She gave him a hug. "You're the best, Giovanni. Marrying Enrico, I've gained a brother. There isn't anything we wouldn't do for you."

"I'll remember that." He hugged her back.

They parted and went different ways. She returned to the apartment to wait for Enrico. He came in two minutes after.

"Donetta?" He swung her around. "We're going back to our camp. I need time alone with you away from the palace. Pack what you need and let's get going."

Life with Enrico was one of total excitement. She threw a few things together and they left in the Jaguar. She looked up at the sky. It was semi-cloudy and she could tell the clouds were gathering. Donetta wouldn't be surprised if there was a rainstorm by dark.

After they reached the mountains, there was still some sun. They changed into their swimming gear and walked out on the sandbar. So much had happened since the moment Enrico had left their apartment last evening that she could hardly believe it.

He leaned over her to give her a long, sensuous kiss. "This afternoon we achieved *détente*."

"Incredible, isn't it? She told me to call her Mamma."

"I knew she would in time."

"Did you honestly think that dangling the

'queen' carrot in front of me was what it took for me to say yes to you?"

Enrico let out a deep sigh. "I didn't know, but I wasn't about to take the chance of losing you if it would convince you to say yes to me."

"When you kissed me the first time, my sixteen-year-old heart knew I wanted to marry you. If you'd asked me to visit you at Cambridge, I would have been on the next plane and never gone home."

"Donetta—"

"It's true. Yesterday was a revelation to me when you introduced me to the leadership in your office. In my naivety growing up, I thought that changing the law of succession in Domodossola would be a snap and all I had to do was get my father to present it to the legislature.

"But with every word of that speech you gave your legislature, I saw their shock and consternation, not just your mother's. For the first time I understood for myself that you don't change a law that has run a country like yours or my family's for centuries without bringing on a civil war. That's what would have happened with your cabinet.

"Do you have any idea how much I love you for trying to do that for me? But I don't want to run your country with you. I never did! What I want to do is be there with you and for you when you need me.

"I'll always help you in any way I can, but you're the acting king. Your people love and respect you like I do. The only reason I married you is because I *love* you. Can we start over again, *amore mio*?"

At this point Enrico was having trouble taking this all in. He had no words, only love he needed to lavish on her. He took her inside and followed her down on the bed where he could devour her. His sweet, passionate wife showed him so much love that by the time they became aware of their surroundings hours later, the rain had started.

"It's a good thing we came in when we did and missed the cloudburst," he whispered against her throat.

She burrowed against him. "There's been another kind of burst in here. I'm so in love with you. There's no one like you in this whole world and I can't do enough to show you how I feel."

He crushed her to him. "I owe Giovanni for bringing us together so fast."

"I love him. We have to do something wonderful for him."

"Tomorrow we'll go back and free him of all responsibilities for a good month. We have an apartment in London where he can stay. He has friends there he enjoys."

"Girls, too, I hope."

"Of course. There was one I know he liked. What he needs is the chance to get something going with her."

"I agree."

"Right now I need the rest of the night to believe that you've come back to me. Give me a minute to raid the cooler. We need something to eat before I have my way with you again."

Her laughter was the most beautiful sound he'd ever heard.

Three months later

Donetta was in their apartment getting ready when Lanza and Fausta knocked on the door and came in.

"Oh—" They both gasped in awe at the same time.

"Your coronation gown is perfection itself," Lanza cried out.

"It's the same gown I was married in. Enrico asked me to wear it, but we had it altered to add the train."

"You look like Cinderella at the ball."

The reference to Cinderella made her smile, reminding her of a certain conversation with Giovanni. "Do you have any idea how much I envy you? You look adorable pregnant. I bet Stefano can't keep his hands off you."

"Donetta—"

Fausta laughed. "I was just about to say the same thing. This is one exciting day." She turned to Donetta. "You do look incredible, sister dear. Enrico will be speechless when he sees you. Only a woman with your coloring and figure could possibly carry it off. Forgive me if I say you look like a queen?"

They all laughed at the insider joke. "Thank you, but I'm the one who'll lose it when we walk down the aisle and Enrico is crowned king. Honestly, he's so gorgeous in his ceremonial suit I die every time I look at him. I'm just thankful his mother decided the coronation could take place."

Lanza eyed her with concern. "Is his father worse?"

"He's slowly failing physically, but I believe she's trying to make up for the way she treated Enrico when we first got married."

Fausta smiled. "I take it all is well now."

"Things couldn't be better. Guess what? Giovanni told me a secret. He said Enrico made another speech to his cabinet that he was so in love with me that he'd wanted to impress me and give me power I didn't have. They all laughed, thinking it was a great joke. They'll never know what we've been through, but that's all right because everything is running beautifully."

Lanza opened the door of the apartment for her. "We'd better go downstairs to the limo, Donetta. Your husband will be waiting for you at the cathedral."

As the three of them left, Fausta said, "To think there was a time when you didn't want to get married."

"Don't remind me. I can't believe I was ever that stupid. While this subject is under discussion, maybe you should reexamine your desire to marry a commoner."

"Why did you just say that?"

"I don't know. Remember the old adage? *Be careful what you wish for.*"

"Donetta—"

"Don't mind me. I'm so happy I don't know what I'm saying."

"Shall we go?"

Within minutes the limo whisked them away to the cathedral.

Donetta was stunned by its beauty. She could hear the organ and choir as they entered the doors. While her sisters joined their mother inside, Donetta joined her father.

He wore his ceremonial dress suit and sash, looking kingly and splendid as always. She was afraid he was worn out, but he seemed to be handling all the festivities very well.

They walked arm in arm down the aisle toward the cardinal in his red robes. The grandeur of these surroundings made the experience surreal.

Their families were seated on carved chairs on one side, facing the aisle. Queen Teodora wore a cream-colored gown. Next to her, King Nuncio sat in his wheelchair. He was dressed in his ceremonial finery and no longer wore a cast. Enrico's sisters sat by him, along with their husbands and Prince Giovanni.

Donetta's mother wore blue chiffon. Her sisters were dressed in their lavender gowns. Lanza sat close to her handsome husband, Stefano. They all looked spectacular.

Holding on to her father, Donetta walked to the front, where King Victor helped her to sit in the carved chair next to the one Enrico would occupy. Then he took his seat next to her mother.

Enrico came in through a side door at the front to join her. He was dressed in his ceremonial navy blue suit with gold epaulets on the shoulders and his light blue sash. If Donetta were the type to swoon from such unmatchable male beauty—an old-fashioned word—she would have fallen at his feet in a white lace heap.

Today her husband was being proclaimed king. He looked so handsome and splendid she could hardly breathe. How blessed was she to be his wife and lover. No woman could be as insanely in love as she was.

Enrico's black eyes met hers and flashed. *He* knew exactly what was running through her private thoughts, and she blushed.

Like in everything he did, Enrico had been thoughtful, asking the cardinal to keep the coronation short enough to accommodate both their fathers, who shouldn't have to endure anything lengthy.

She'd learned that the cardinal was an old friend of their family, eager to comply with Enrico's wishes. The speech about anointing the king didn't take long. After his solemn talk, they were instructed to pray, and the choir sang a gorgeous piece of music.

Donetta was overjoyed when the cardinal picked up the crown and placed it on Enrico's head. No man in existence could match her husband for his striking presence or inner goodness.

Her heart turned over on itself when Enrico reached for her hand so she could stand next to him. "Just wait until later," he whispered in her ear, sending darts of awareness to the tips of her fingers.

The cardinal blessed both of them before the organ burst forth and they heard bells ringing. Donetta was excited beyond belief

when they walked down the aisle to the en-
closed carriage waiting outside. Their ride
would end at the palace with a feast awaiting
everyone in the main dining room.

Once he released her, they turned to their
families. To her everlasting gratitude, everyone showed a surfeit of love today. As for
Enrico's mother, her decision to allow the
coronation to proceed made Donetta love her
more than ever.

Back at the palace, Enrico removed the
crown and the festivities began. Their coronation dinner included champagne toasts
from everyone, including Enrico's sisters.
Donetta loved all the tributes, especially the
ones from Fausta and Giovanni, who'd sat together and seemed to be enjoying each other's company. They stood at the same time
and revealed secrets back and forth to everyone's amusement.

"To my cousin Enrico, whom I've never
seen so happy in my life. Every time he had
a date with a girl, I'd ask him if he was going
to see her again, but he'd say he wasn't interested. I couldn't figure out what was wrong
until he finally told me about Donetta. And

then we planned the *concorso* here so she'd come."

"That explains everything," Fausta blurted. "To Donetta! If you've all noticed, she's glowing. When she returned home from that competition, I never saw anyone so happy. She told me Enrico had taken her on a picnic. I knew she was crazy about him.

"She reminds me of Lanza who came back from their last trip to Argentina and told us she and Stefano were expecting a baby."

Everyone laughed and clapped in delight. Knowing Lanza was going to have a son very soon made this coronation day extra special for Donetta.

Her father made the last toast. "To my beloved daughter Donetta. I couldn't agree with your sister more. I've never known you to be this happy, which means you've met the right man in Enrico. May you always feel this same joy through the years and know the contentment I've had with my bride."

His toast brought tears to Donetta's eyes and her mother's. She glanced at Enrico's mother. How hard this had to be for her because of her husband's illness. Enrico had to be thinking the same thing. He squeezed

Donetta's hip before leaving her side to go hug his mother and father.

His devotion to them made Donetta love her new husband with a fierceness she didn't know herself capable of. Later in the day he stole her away and they hurried to their apartment where they could be alone at last.

He kissed her long and hard. "Let's hurry and get changed. I have a surprise for you."

"You do too much for me already," Donetta murmured against his lips.

"This is a small thing, but I know you'll enjoy it. Wear something casual."

"Life is always exciting with you."

She rushed to get out of the gown she'd worn to the coronation, wondering if he wanted to go on a horseback ride or some such thing.

In a few minutes they were both ready. He'd dressed in cargo pants and a sports shirt. From king to sailor, he was equally gorgeous.

Donetta smiled at him. "Before we leave, I have two surprises for you."

"You do?" He looked excited.

"One is in here. Come into the living room." She reached for his hand and walked him out of their bedroom. "Look over on the far wall."

Those black eyes swerved in that direction. She felt his body quicken as he pulled her with him to the oil painting of his latest horse.

She knew she'd given him something he would cherish. He crushed her to him. "It's fabulous."

"Just like you."

"I adore you, *bellissima*."

After another lengthy kiss they left the apartment and hurried down the staircase to the entrance where he kept his Jaguar. Was he taking them back to their camp?

But her question was answered quickly when he drove down to the lake and parked at a pier, where she saw a gleaming white sailboat moored.

She squealed when she noticed the name on the side and turned to him. "You've named it the *Luna*!"

"That's right. When I decided to buy this sailboat, I had you in mind. But I didn't want to give away my secret and call it *Donetta*. Your horse's name was the next best choice.

"The day you won that championship on

Luna was years ago, but I recognized there was something special about you even back then. You have no idea how excited I am to be sleeping on board with my wife who was once a girl with hair like a silvery gold waterfall."

She launched herself in his arms. This was love beyond imagining. He walked her down the pier and helped her onto the boat.

The sun was about to disappear below the horizon. She looked into his eyes. "Now it's time to tell you about my second gift. I haven't seen a doctor yet, but I did a home test and—"

"I've made you pregnant already?" he cried. The elation in his voice told her everything she wanted to know. *Donetta!*

"Won't it be fun to see if we have a boy with my color of hair or a girl with yours? You'll make the most wonderful father in the whole world."

Enrico rocked her in his arms, apparently too overcome to talk, and they lay together, looking forward to their wonderful future.

* * * * *